Her Man of Honor

TERI WILSON

HARLEQUIN

SPECIAL
EDITION

ISBN-13: 978-1-335-72456-4

Her Man of Honor

Recycling programs for this product may not exist in your area.

For questions and comments about the quality of this book, please contact us at CustomerService@Harlequin.com.

Harlequin Enterprises ULC
22 Adelaide St. West, 41st Floor
Toronto, Ontario M5H 4E3, Canada
www.Harlequin.com

Printed in U.S.A.

USA TODAY bestselling author **Teri Wilson** writes heartwarming romance for Harlequin Special Edition. Three of Teri's books have been adapted into Hallmark Channel Original Movies, most notably *Unleashing Mr. Darcy*. She is also a recipient of the prestigious RITA® Award for excellence in romantic fiction and a recent inductee into the San Antonio Women's Hall of Fame.

Teri has a special fondness for cute dogs and pretty dresses, and she loves following the British royal family. Visit her at www.teriwilson.net.

Books by Teri Wilson

Harlequin Special Edition

Lovestruck, Vermont

Baby Lessons
Firehouse Christmas Baby
The Trouble with Picket Fences

Furever Yours

How to Rescue a Family
A Double Dose of Happiness

Montana Mavericks: Six Brides for Six Brothers

The Maverick's Secret Baby

Love, Unveiled

Her Man of Honor

Visit the Author Profile page
at Harlequin.com for more titles.

In loving memory of my grandmother
Peggy McNamara Wilson

Chapter One

Accoording to her sister, Everly England had been waiting her entire life to wear Marchesa.

Addison always credited Everly's childhood Disney princess obsession for putting visions of frothy ball gowns in her head, but truthfully, her adult life had much more to do with it. As a columnist for *Veil*, Manhattan's premiere bridal magazine, Everly was immersed in chiffon and sequins on an almost daily basis. So *of course* she had opinions about what she'd wear when her big day finally came. And yes, as Addison predicted, she chose Marchesa—a romantic masterpiece of a gown with a lace bodice and full tulle skirt covered with delicate lace flower appliqués and a pale pink satin bow tied at the waist.

Cinderella would have been proud.

There was only one problem. In all of Everly's fantasies involving the wedding dress of her dreams, she saw herself standing beside Gregory, the love of her life. She'd envisioned the wedding so many times that the tiniest details were ingrained in her head, as if they'd already taken place—the exchanging of vows, the first kiss, the cutting of the cake.

It had all gone so smoothly in her imagination. So elegantly, like one of the stunning pictorials *Veil* was so famous for. Never once had Everly pictured her gorgeous designer gown billowing around her in a dejected puff as she sat cross-legged on the bathroom floor of the Plaza Hotel's honeymoon suite. Alone.

Yet, there she was.

She tried not to think about the towering white cake from Ron Ben-Israel sitting untouched downstairs in the Terrace room as she reached for another cracker and topped it with a generous dose of squirt cheese. As if the indignity of being left at the altar wasn't bad enough, she was eating cheese from a can. Who knew they even sold something so deliciously pathetic in the Plaza gift shop?

The skirt of her exquisite Marchesa was littered with cracker crumbs, and Everly couldn't have cared less. Where was Gregory? And why had he waited until they were standing hand in hand in front of all their nearest and dearest as well as photographers from both *Veil* and the *New York Times* to decide that he didn't want to marry her after all?

She probably should have seen it coming. Scratch that—she definitely should have known something was wrong. Everly was, after all, a bona fide expert on love and relationships. She'd been writing the Lovebirds column at *Veil* for nearly three years now. Every month she answered letters from nervous brides-to-be, dishing out advice about everything from what to do when the groom showed zero interest in choosing flower arrangements to how often an engaged couple should be sleeping together.

That last one was always tricky. Planning a wedding was a stressful time, and every couple was different. But somehow Everly sensed that four straight months of abstinence wasn't the norm. If a bride had written her a letter describing the bedroom situation between Everly and Gregory leading up to the ceremony, she would have found a way to delicately suggest counseling. Or at the very least a candid heart-to-heart.

How could she have been so blind?

She topped another cracker with a generous swirl of canned cheese, and just as she was about to bite into it, her cell phone blared to life. It vibrated across the polished tile floor as her wedding march ring tone filled the air. *Ugh.*

She glanced at the little screen. Addison again. Everly knew she should answer it, but she just couldn't face the *Veil* crew. Not now. Addison was her sister, but as deputy editor, she was also Everly's boss. Their close friend and third member of their girl squad, Daphne, also worked at *Veil* as the beauty editor. Working with family and friends had always been one of Everly's favorite parts about her job. Every Thursday night, she, Addison and Daphne got together for happy hour to dish about the office and dream about the day Addison would be promoted and the three of them would take over the magazine. They had so many plans…fabulous plans, *big* plans.

Unfortunately, none of those plans included Everly making a huge joke out of her column.

Or her life in general.

She banged out a quick text assuring Addison she was fine and just needed some space, then switched her phone to silent and flipped it facedown on the tile. For once, *Veil* was the furthest thing from her mind. What was she supposed to do now? She couldn't hide in the honeymoon suite for the rest of her life. The Plaza had comped the room for one night, which was one of the generous perks of working for a bridal magazine. Checkout was at eleven in the morning, though, and Everly didn't even know where her overnight bag was. She was going to have to walk-of-shame it out of the hotel onto Central Park South in her wedding gown and hail a cab home.

Lovely.

She blinked back tears as she reached, yet again, for the can of cheese. But then a knock sounded on the hotel room door and she froze, mid-squirt.

Good grief, her sister was relentless. Couldn't she and Daphne take a hint and give her half a second to absorb the fact that everything she'd believed in for the past two years had apparently been a big, fat lie? When had Gregory stopped loving her? Had he *ever* loved her to begin with?

Everly bit down hard on her bottom lip to keep from sobbing out loud. Maybe if she stayed very still and very quiet, they'd give up and go away so she could have her breakdown in private.

The pounding on the door resumed, louder this time. Privacy was a pipe dream, apparently.

Everly's head fell back against the bathroom's grand, opulent tub, and she groaned, "Would you please stop before someone calls security?"

She dragged herself off the floor and made her way to the door in a trail of tulle and lace, canned cheese in hand. The only thing that would make this situation even more awkward would be the addition of a starched Plaza security officer. So she took a deep breath, braced herself for the sight of Addison and Daphne in their bridesmaids' gowns and swung the door open.

"Hey." Henry Aston, Everly's closest friend outside the *Veil* girls, arched a brow as his gaze homed in on the can in her hand. "Wow. You know all those fancy wedding hors d'oeuvres you and what's-his-name picked out are being passed around in the ballroom, right? I could fix you a plate and bring it up. The avocado crostini is fantastic."

What's-his-name. Everly couldn't help but smile through her tears. Despite the fact that Henry spent more time on airplanes than he did in his West Village apartment, he definitely knew Gregory well enough to remember his name.

"Thanks, but no." She didn't want any part of the wedding food, even the posh homage to her beloved avocado toast that she'd been so excited about adding to the menu.

She didn't want any part of the wedding, *period.* Not even the dress. She'd be wrapped in a terry cloth Plaza bathrobe right now if she could have managed to unlace the back of her Marchesa by herself.

"Got it. It probably wouldn't pair well with Easy Cheese anyway." Henry shrugged a single muscular tuxedo-clad shoulder. "This might, though."

From behind his back, he produced an unopened bottle of champagne with a pink foil label—a much coveted Dom Pérignon Rosé. Another perk of working for *Veil*.

"The magazine sent that over for the toast. Just one bottle." The guests were getting a more reasonably priced label. This was bottle was special. The thick glass had even been engraved *For the Lovebirds, from your Veil Family.* Everly narrowed her gaze. "How did you manage to get your hands on that?"

"Opening this sucker suddenly seemed more crucial than ever. I have my ways. Isn't that why I'm here?" He reached to give the pink ribbon at her waist an affectionate tug as if the delicate sash were a string she'd tied around her finger to remind herself why she'd scheduled the ceremony around his ridiculously busy travel schedule.

He's your friend.

Your best *friend.*

And right now, he was proving himself to be one heck of a man of honor.

"You can bring that bottle inside under one condition—no wedding talk. None whatsoever." If she wanted to rehash everything that had transpired in the past hour, she'd have answered one of Addison's many calls. Her sister would have been more than happy to talk the nonwedding to death.

Everly didn't want to talk. She just wanted someone to sit quietly beside her and not say a word…to just be there. Henry had always been good at that, even back in college. Eight years ago, on what was undoubtedly the worst night of her life—even worse than this one—he'd parked himself on the floor of her dorm bathroom and held her hand for hours until she finally cried herself to sleep with her head on his shoulder. It had been exactly what she needed.

She looked up at him now, and his gaze softened just enough for her to know he was thinking about that night, too. It was just as raw and real to him as it was to her. Of course it was.

Then he blinked, and she was no longer looking into the eyes of the boy who'd lived across the hall at Columbia. These eyes belonged to someone older. Wiser. All grown up.

"As you wish." He plucked the boutonniere from the lapel of his tuxedo jacket—blue thistle, eucalyptus and soft pink blooms that had already begun to wilt. Then he tossed it over her shoulder, where it landed in the suite's gilded trash can with a whispered thud. "No wedding talk."

Henry began unwrapping the foil on the bottle of Dom as he made his way straight to the bathroom. He didn't bother checking the rest of the luxurious suite for signs of life. No need. He'd known exactly where to find Everly after the wedding had gone bottoms up smack in the middle of the vows.

He'd always known.

Sure enough, a box of Ritz Crackers rested on its side on the slick marble floor, along with her cell phone—encased in silver glitter, because of course—and a generous pile of crumbs. He ground his teeth at the sight of the sad tableau and fought the ever-increasing urge to find Gregory and pound him into the ground. How could he do something like this to her? How could anyone?

Henry wondered briefly if that pathetic jackass

had any idea that Everly liked to hide in bathroom when things in her life went topsy-turvy. He peeled the remaining foil away from the bottle and shook his head. Of course Gregory didn't know. No doubt that was part of the problem.

In the jackass's defense, however, Henry had a feeling Addison wouldn't know where to find her, either. The bathroom thing wasn't something Everly did often—only during the serious storms of her life, like that long ago night at Columbia.

Like now.

The door to the suite clicked shut, and Everly joined him at the his-and-her vanity. Her dress seemed to take up half the room. Henry was no fashion aficionado, but from the moment he'd first set eyes on her in that delicate, ethereal cupcake of a wedding gown, he'd had a strange pang in his chest. She looked beautiful. Everly had *always* been beautiful, but something about the way she looked today was…different. Special.

Then the strangest thing had happened. Henry had watched her walk down the aisle toward the jackass, and the pang in his chest had blossomed into a full-on ache.

What. The. Hell?

This was *Everly*, for crying out loud. She was his friend. Not just any friend, but the closest friend he had in the world. He shouldn't be aching around her.

Nor should he feel oddly hollow at the thought of her marrying another man, and yet...

He had.

And although he'd never admit as much in a million years, Henry's initial reaction when Gregory had bailed on Everly mid-ceremony had been one of stone-cold relief.

What in God's name was wrong with him?

You're the man of honor, remember?

Merriam-Webster invaded his thoughts. *Honor: a keen sense of ethical conduct. See also—integrity.*

He blinked. Hard. Then he caught Everly's gaze in the reflection of the huge mirror above the vanity. Her eyes were glassy. Her irises bright violet—even brighter than usual. She'd been crying.

Somehow, someway, Henry would fix this mess. He had to. That's why he was here. Friendship aside, he'd been somewhat surprised when Everly had called and asked him to be her man of honor. He didn't know the first thing about planning a bridal shower or throwing a bachelorette party or whatever else a proper maid of honor like Addison or Daphne would surely do. For the majority of the engagement, work had prevented him from being anywhere near Manhattan.

But he was here now, and no way was he going to let her down. Whatever weirdness he'd felt earlier had passed. His best friend was falling apart. She *needed* him.

With a twist of his wrist, the cork popped out of the rose-gold bottle of champagne. Everly didn't even flinch. She just stared blankly ahead, and Henry hated Gregory even more for what he'd put her through in front of her family, friends and co-workers. Hell, half of Manhattan had been there to witness it.

"I'll go get some glasses." He turned to head for the suite's minibar, but before he could navigate his way past *the dress*, Everly took the Dom from his hands.

"No need." She took a swig straight from the bottle.

He arched a brow. "Are you going to share, or shall I order another from room service?"

Somehow, that seemed like a bad idea. Monumentally bad.

"We can share." She handed it back to him.

He took a drink while she plopped onto the floor in a pile of bridal white fluff.

"I have to say—" Henry sat down next to her and examined the bottle's pink foil label. "—I know this stuff is pricey, but it lives up to the hype."

"Only the best from *Veil*." Everly sighed. "Too bad I probably won't be working there anymore come Monday."

He passed the bottle to her. "You don't seriously think they'll fire you. What happened just now wasn't your fault."

She swallowed another gulp of rosé. "I'm supposed to be the love and relationships expert, and I just got left at the altar. You have to admit it's not a good look for the magazine."

"Addison will stick up for you. You know that. She'd never let Colette fire you over this." He studied her as she topped a cracker with a generous swirl of cheese. "Besides, we both know your job isn't the most pressing thing on your mind right now."

She handed him the cracker and gave him a watery smile. "Do we?"

Henry gave her a meaningful look until she took a deep breath and nodded.

"I just don't understand what happened." Her bottom lip began to quiver so much that Henry had to ball his hands into fists to keep from reaching to still it with a gentle press of his fingertips. "He left me…on our *wedding* day. I should have seen it coming. I…"

"Stop." His voice echoed off the tile, and she flinched. "I repeat—this was *not* your fault, E. Tell me you understand that."

She blinked, then her eyes filled, and the tremble in her bottom lip grew so fierce that he couldn't take it anymore and had to look away. He stared into the opening of the champagne bottle for a long silent moment.

Everly sniffled beside him.

He took a long pull from the bottle, releasing it only when the bubbles caused his eyes to water.

"You're the most loyal person I know," he said. His voice was suddenly a raw, aching thing, and he told himself it was a result of the champagne, not any lingering, inappropriate feelings. But on some deep, forbidden level, he knew better than to believe it. "Loyal to a fault."

"Loyal." She took a deep, shuddering inhale. "But not *desirable*."

By some miracle, Henry stopped his head from whipping around to gape at her. What in the world was she talking about? "Did Gregory tell you that?"

"He didn't have to." Everly's voice was as small and quiet as he'd ever heard it, but it somehow reached deep into his chest and stoked the ache he'd been doing his best to ignore. "We haven't slept together in over four months."

"E…" He searched her gaze.

He wasn't sure he should be hearing this.

Actually, he was certain he *shouldn't*. Not when her almost-wedding had tied him up in knots and not when she was so broken, so vulnerable.

So *close*.

"Never mind." She shook her head, and her cheeks flared pink. "Forget I said anything."

He wished he could. Impossible. No effing way.

"Listen to me, sweetheart." He reached for her face and with gentle fingertips, urged her to turn and meet his gaze. "You are most definitely desirable."

"You think?" Her gaze dropped to his mouth.

Henry stopped breathing for a second as something strange and new percolated between them. Alarm bells were going off in every corner of his mind, even as his body went as hard as granite.

It took every ounce of self-control in his arsenal to tear his gaze away from those beautiful eyes he knew so well—eyes that were suddenly looking at him with a yearning that mirrored everything he'd been feeling for the past few hours.

Longer than that, if he was really being honest with himself.

"I *know*, E," he whispered, struggling to keep his tone as neutral and friendly as possible.

Her sudden intake of breath told him it was a wasted effort.

"Henry," she said. "Would you…"

She was going to ask him to kiss her. The question floated between them in a swirl of history and close calls and missed opportunities. A bond had formed between them on that night back in college, and at first, it had been so sacred he was hesitant to act on it. What they had was too important to risk over a dumb spur-of-the-moment decision to give into temptation and kiss her. By the time he realized the urge wasn't going to go away, she'd gone and gotten herself a boyfriend. Months later, when that relationship had ended, Henry had already begun dating someone else. A nice girl—pretty and bubbly, perfect in every way except one.

She wasn't Everly.

The past eight years had been the same kind of roller coaster ride. Henry and Everly had never been simultaneously single and on the same continent until now...on what was supposed to be her wedding night.

He closed his eyes. *Don't do it.*

What kind of cad would he be if he made his move now? The worst possible kind. But before the words *man of dishonor* could form in his mind, Everly's lips brushed against his—hesitant, soft and full of questions he'd been asking himself for the better part of eight years.

Henry's eyes fluttered and he squinted, letting the light in. He had to put a stop to things, now, before it was too late. One glance was all it took, though. The air shimmered with heat, glittering around them brighter and more brilliant than the diamond on Everly's finger. He felt like he was looking at his best friend for the very first time.

And then she kissed him again with eyes wide open.

Chapter Two

The first thing Everly saw when she opened her eyes the following morning was her wedding gown lying in a forgotten heap on the floor by the foot of the bed. She frowned at it, somewhat surprised she hadn't bothered to hang it up. Granted, after yesterday she never wanted to see it again, but still. Thanks to her position at *Veil*, she'd gotten the dress on loan from the fashion house. The ridiculously expensive gown didn't actually belong to her, and there it was on the floor of the Plaza's honeymoon suite, looking as if it had been trampled by a herd of elephants.

The whole room was kind of a mess, really. Rose petals littered every surface in her line of vision—the nightstand, the coffee table, the minibar. Her attention lingered on the bar, where sunlight streaming through the suite's floor-to-ceiling windows glinted off the rose-gold label of a champagne bottle. Why did it suddenly feel as if Dom Pérignon himself was winking at her?

She closed her eyes for a moment, certain she was dreaming. Scenes from the night before flashed through her mind like some kind of madcap romantic comedy on Netflix. When the pictures veered into naughty territory starring none other than her *best friend* Henry Aston, Everly's eyes flew open.

Stop it.

She shouldn't be having those kind of dreams about Henry—especially when she was supposed to be on a cruise ship to the Bahamas right now with Gregory. It wasn't until her gaze landed on a wisp of pale blue satin and lace beside the pretty pink bottle that she realized she hadn't been dreaming at all.

Her eyes widened in alarm.

What were her *panties*—her carefully chosen something blue—doing on the minibar? And why on earth was there a black silk satin bow tie dangling from the edge of the counter right beside them?

Who even wore self-tied bow ties anymore, other than George Clooney? Granted, Everly loved them. But for all their retro charm, they were always a little asymmetrical. Never quite perfect. According to a *Veil* feature from a few months ago, more than ninety percent of bow ties in modern weddings were pre-tied. Case in point—Gregory's had been pre-tied, pressed to perfection by the geniuses at Ralph Lauren.

But Gregory wasn't here, obviously. Much to Everly's dismay, neither was George Clooney. When she finally sat up and inspected the other half of the bed, she found Henry stretched out beside her.

Henry.

Very drowsy, very handsome and very, *very* naked.

Oh.

My.

Gosh.

Those naughty dreams about him had been real. *Everything* had been real—from the hand-holding to the kissing to the begging. Ugh, the begging!

After she'd kissed him, she'd come right out and asked him to make love to her. Being the trustworthy, good man that Henry was, he'd turned her down. So she'd asked him again…a couple of times.

And then she'd begged.

That had finally done the trick. Now here he was, as naked as the day he was born.

She took a deep breath and tried to drag her gaze away from his finely sculpted abs, slim hips and… *gulp*…everything else. When had Henry gotten so muscular? He'd looked nothing like this in college. He'd been slim as a reed—bookish and quiet. A dreamer, just like her.

Not so slim anymore, apparently. Henry had been crisscrossing the globe for the past few years writing for *Wanderlust*, a popular online travel magazine based in the UK. All that time spent backpacking through Australia and snorkeling off the coast of Fiji had clearly left its mark.

It was strange seeing him like this. The sight of his sun-kissed skin, darkly elegant against the crisp white bed sheets, made Everly a little breathless, which was probably silly, considering everything they'd done the night before.

But so much of last night was a frenzied blur. There had been far too much sensation for Everly to focus on anything particular, and now she felt like she was starving for details. The heat of his lips on her neck. His calloused hands on the tender flesh of her thighs. The taste of him—lush and exotic, wildly different than what she'd always imagined.

Because yes, she'd thought about sleeping with Henry before last night. Of course she had. How could she not? He was the best man she'd ever known. And yes, maybe a tiny part of her had always been in love with him. Gregory had certainly thought so, but Everly had never entertained the possibility of an actual affair with Henry. He was too important to her. She couldn't risk losing him as a friend, so she'd always pretended not to notice the butterflies that took flight in her belly every time he breezed back into Manhattan from whatever corner of the world had most recently claimed him.

So much for self-restraint.

She blinked back tears as she took in his languid, sleeping form. As much as he'd changed, he was still the same old Henry. He'd still known where to find her when her life was in tatters. He'd still known the exact right things to say.

Listen to me, sweetheart. You are most definitely desirable.

Somehow, in the blink of an eye, he'd gone from being something old to becoming something new. And it scared the wits out of her. It frightened her so badly that when she tried to imagine what she'd possibly say to him when he woke up that she let out a panicked little whimper.

The corner of Henry's lips twitched, and she clamped a hand over her mouth. Perfect. She'd gone and roused him.

"Good morning," he said without opening his eyes. The timbre of his voice was lower than she'd ever heard it before—intimate in a way that made her heart feel like it was being squeezed in a vise.

She couldn't do this.

Mere hours ago, she'd been left at the altar. Jilted brides weren't supposed to fall into bed with a member of the wedding party. She should be home right now returning bridal gifts and plotting Gregory's demise. Better yet, she should be following the kind of advice she dished out in her column. Just last August, Everly had answered a letter from a bride who'd been ditched at the altar and had urged her to take time for self-care and reflection. She'd prescribed sheet masks, herbal tea and a weekend away at a spa. Not once had she advised the bride to hook up with the first willing stranger she came across.

Henry wasn't a stranger, obviously. He was her best friend, which made her decision to jump his bones even more foolish. She felt like her heart was outside of her body right now, lying on the petal-strewn bed between them. All she wanted to do was put it back where it belonged…to protect it before another horrible wave of rejection came her way. She could take losing Gregory, but she'd never survive losing Henry.

There was only one way to make sure that never, ever happened.

"Morning," she said stiffly, scurrying out of the bed in desperate search of one of the white terry cloth robes emblazoned with the Plaza's crest she'd seen hanging in the bathroom closet the night before.

Step one: stop being naked.

Step two: admit last night had been a terrible mistake that should never, ever be repeated.

She yanked the belt of the bathrobe tight as she walked back into bedroom, pausing only slightly at the sight of Henry sitting up, awake now. And still very exposed.

"Here." She offered him the matching robe from the his-and-her set.

Please, please put it on. It was her only hope. She'd

never be able to pretend she regretted last night if she had to do it while staring at those abs.

Henry's gaze flitted to the robe and then back at her.

"Thanks," he said quietly. Then he raked a hand through his hair as he climbed out of bed to put it on.

He looked so charmingly rumpled, just like a man who'd spent all night rolling around in a bed in one of Manhattan's finest luxury hotels. Which he had… with *her*.

How was any of this possible?

She turned around while he slipped into the robe, staring fixedly at the bottle on the minibar so she wouldn't be tempted to sneak one last look at his impossibly hot body in one of the room's mirrored surfaces. They'd emptied less than half the bottle. Great. She couldn't even blame her startling lack of judgment on the champagne.

"Listen, E…" Henry started, and when she turned back around, he was looking at her with the same lopsided smile she'd known and loved for nearly a decade.

But it wasn't the same smile. He wasn't the same gangly bookish boy who loved the planetarium and street pretzels, and who'd gamely watched *Breakfast at Tiffany's* with her at least two dozen times. *They* weren't the same, and thanks to last night, they never would be again.

Their eyes met. Held. And for a second, Everly

thought about closing the space between them and kissing him hard on the mouth, running her finger-tips over his scruffy, chiseled face and falling back onto the soft, luxurious hotel bed. They could make love again and then order room service and do the *New York Times* crossword together. Everly thought she just might be perfectly happy to spend the rest of her life right here in the Plaza's honeymoon suite.

With him.

But then Henry's smile turned sad around the edges. Bittersweet. And Everly felt like her entire chest was caving in on itself.

"I'm sorry," he said. "Last night, I…"

She shook her head. *No. No, no, no.* "Please don't say anything."

He walked toward her, all mussed hair and famil-iar warmth, and it took every last shred of Everly's dignity not to bury her face in his shoulder and cry.

This couldn't be happening. Everly had heard him talk about this exact speech before. She'd helped him perfect it, in fact. *Start out by saying you're sorry,* she'd told him when he'd been trying to figure out what to do about a woman at work who'd developed a crush on him. He'd wanted to let her down gently, because that's the sort of stand-up guy Henry was. Everly had given the same advice she would've given anyone who'd submitted a question to her Lovebirds column at *Veil.* And now here she was, on the receiv-ing end of her very own "let her down gently" script.

Hearing those words come out of Henry's mouth would be the final straw. Everly would rather walk down Madison Avenue stark naked during Fashion Week than let him finish.

She took a step back, out of his reach.

"Let's just pretend last night never happened, okay? And let's definitely not talk about it." She tried to swallow, but a lump the size of the Empire State Building had lodged itself in her throat. "*Ever.*"

"But, E…"

She wished he'd stop calling her that. *E* had always been Henry's special nickname for her. No one else used it—not even Gregory. For college graduation, Henry had given her a sterling silver necklace from Tiffany's, with a dainty E charm that came to rest gently in the dip between her collar bones. She'd worn it nearly every day since…until Gregory had replaced it with a large, ostentatious diamond from Harry Winston.

As if he could read her mind, Henry's gaze dropped to the glittering stone. A muscle in his jaw ticked.

Everly pulled her bathrobe tighter around her form. She wished she could simply disappear in that plush terry cloth like a turtle retreating into its shell. "It was a crazy mistake. We both lost our heads. Honestly, you don't have to say anything."

Henry's jaw visibly clenched. "You're sure?"

"Positive." Everly nodded and pasted on a smile. If she kept looking him in the eyes, that fixed smile would wobble straight off her face, so she focused on his forehead instead. His handsome, handsome forehead.

Ugh, she had it bad, didn't she? Since when were foreheads a magnet for sexual attraction?

"Okay then," Henry said.

Everly nodded. "Okay then."

They were on the same page, just like always. Henry Aston wasn't her something new. He wasn't even her something old. Not anymore. He was her something borrowed...

Just for a night.

Henry stood beside Everly in one of the Plaza's opulent elevators and did his best not to stare at her bare porcelain shoulders in the gilded mirror directly across from them. Or the tender curve of her neck. Or the place just below her left ear where she loved to be kissed.

Last night, when he'd pressed his lips to that spot, she'd purred like a kitten. All softness and warmth. Henry's only coherent thought had been *Finally*. Their friendship had always been the one constant in his adult life—the only true, pure thing he knew he could always count on. The moment he'd pushed inside her last night had seemed predestined, as if every second they'd spent together over the years had been leading up to that blissful moment in time.

Everly had always been his compass, and after so much wandering, he'd finally come home.

Then the sun had come up, and here they were, back in their wedding clothes. Back to being best friends.

The elevator lurched and Henry's stomach lurched along with it. His hastily consumed cup of coffee sloshed to and fro, causing bile to rise up the back of his throat. After dropping the "let's not talk about it…ever" bomb on him, Everly had promptly disappeared back to her refuge. The bathroom.

This time, Henry had known better than to follow. Instead, he'd ordered coffee from room service, which had come in an elegant silver pot with two china cups instead of a vat where he could simply dunk his head, as he'd so desperately needed. He'd barely taken a swallow when Everly had emerged wearing her wedding gown and announced she was ready to check out.

Henry hadn't expected to see her for at least an hour. He'd imagined her submersed in warm bubbles with her hair twisted on top of her head in the massive marble tub. Everly was the biggest bubble bath enthusiast he'd ever met, and that tub was straight out of her dreams…a bathtub built for two.

"You're sure?" he'd asked. Again. It was all he could seem to say this morning, in the wake of what she obviously considered an enormous mistake.

"Yes," she'd said without quite meeting his gaze.

That mistake was the best damn night of my life.

This was all his fault. He should've known it wasn't the right time. She'd been vulnerable, and he'd been knocked sideways by the sight of her on the verge of becoming one with another man. If he'd had a shred of self-control last night—if he'd acted in any way close to honorably—they wouldn't be here right now. They'd be sitting cross-legged on the luxe bed in the honeymoon suite eating room service pancakes and watching one of Everly's comfort shows. *Breakfast at Tiffany's*, for the ten millionth time. Or maybe her other perennial favorite *Friends*. Henry would do his Chandler Bing impression, and Everly would snort-laugh even though she'd heard it a million times before. Henry had always been the only one who could make her laugh like that. Cheeky and loud, with her head tossed back and her thick, dark hair spilling down her slender back.

But Henry hadn't acted honorably. He accepted full responsibility for the fact their friendship had veered completely off the rail, so when she'd insisted she wanted to go, he'd bitten his tongue and tossed back the rest of the coffee in a single gulp.

It burned like hell all the way down.

"E, there's something I need to tell you," he said, locking eyes with her in the elevator mirror.

Her mascara was smudged, and her lips were lush and swollen from all that had gone on the night before. What was left of her neat bridal updo was a half-up, half-down, tousled mass of curls that made him itch to run his fingers through her hair. Again.

He flexed his hands and then closed them into tight fists to prevent himself from doing something stupid, like twirling a lock of that lush hair of hers around his fingertips. Henry had never seen this version of Everly. Sensual…*sated*. It made his throat go thick with a longing so intense that his knees nearly buckled. A forbidden thrill coursed through him at the thought that there were still new things to discover about each other, even after all this time.

Then Everly's eyes grew shiny as amethysts as she gazed back at him, and even though her lips weren't moving, Henry could hear her voice in his head as clear as day.

Let's just pretend last night never happened, okay?

"I told you, you don't need to apologize." She let out a nervous laugh that didn't come close to meeting her eyes. Henry realized, to his horror, that she was on the verge of tears.

"It's not about last night," he said.

She nodded, but he could tell she wasn't listening. She was a million miles away.

Henry sighed. This wasn't how he'd planned on sharing his news. He'd imagined telling her on the dance floor after she'd exchanged vows with Gregory. Or over a fat slice of wedding cake they'd share at the Plaza's Champagne Bar overlooking Fifth Avenue and the Pulitzer Fountain. That should have been Henry's first clue he wasn't ready for her to marry someone else. Brides didn't steal away with their male best friends in the middle of their wedding reception, even when the man of honor had an important announcement to make. The thought that such a scenario had seemed perfectly feasible to Henry should have been a warning sign.

"Don't you have a plane to catch?" Everly asked, dragging his thoughts back to the here and now.

Henry felt himself frown. *Damn it.* He'd forgotten about Bora-Bora. Then again, what else was new? He always had a plane to catch.

He glanced at his watch—a Cartier tank his father had given him for high school graduation. The reverse had been engraved with a Tolkien quote: "Not all those who wander are lost." Henry had seen numerous continents since he'd first strapped that Cartier to his wrist. Five, and counting...

Sometimes he wondered if his dad was up in heaven, tagging along in spirit. He would've been so happy for Henry, so proud. His long battle with lymphoma had ended before Henry had moved into his freshman dorm at Columbia later that fall.

See the world, son. Life is shorter than you could ever imagine. Do it for me, he'd said over and over again during his final days. He'd squeezed Henry's hand with staggering force, and the plea had imprinted itself on Henry's heart as solidly as if it had been engraved there. Forged in the fire of pain and suffering, of a life cut short. Henry's dad had so many plans for his retirement. As soon as he reached sixty-five, he was going to sell the bodega that he ran in Brooklyn and buy an RV. He wanted to see all fifty states by the time he was seventy.

In the end, he'd never left the state of New York.

Henry knew it wasn't logical to blame himself. He'd been just a small boy when his mother walked out, leaving his dad to care for Henry on his own. Even growing up without a mom, he'd never for a moment felt unwanted or unloved. But he wished his father had been given the chance to live his dream. Now there was nothing left to do but live it for him.

"I've got time. My flight doesn't board for two hours." A lie. If he didn't get a cab straight to JFK, he'd have to rearrange his entire itinerary.

"Where to this time?" Everly asked.

"French Polynesia. Specifically, Bora-Bora."

"Sounds nice," she said, and for a second, her mask slipped. The longing he felt deep in his bones seemed to be looking right back at him from the depths of Everly's shimmering violet eyes.

"Come with me," he said. The words left his mouth before he could stop them. He shrugged and did his best to make the invitation sound casual. Only half serious. "You're supposed to be on your honeymoon. You've got the time off. Why not make the most of it?"

Everly's face went as pink as the rose petals from last night's centerpieces. "Don't be ridiculous. I can't just jet off to Bora-Bora…"

With my man of honor.

She didn't say it, but the words floated between them all the same.

"I mean as friends, obviously," he said. They could do this, couldn't they? They could rewind the clock and go back to what they'd been before.

"As friends," she echoed. "Of course."

They didn't dare look directly at one another. They just kept their gazes fixed on their mutual reflections in the elevator's mirrored walls. Everly swallowed, and Henry traced the movement up and down the slender column of her throat. God, she was beautiful. Beautiful, bedazzling and very much *not* his.

The elevator jolted to a stop.

"I really can't," Everly said as the elevators swished open. "I need to stay here and rebuild."

"Rebuild?" Henry arched a brow as he placed his hand on the small of her back and escorted her across the glittering hotel lobby.

"My life," Everly clarified. "Starting with saving my job."

Before Henry could respond, the Plaza's manager on duty came scurrying toward them from the reception desk.

"Good morning to our Plaza newlyweds," he

gushed. Clearly this guy hadn't gotten the memo about what had transpired in the ballroom last night. "Mr. and Mrs. Hoyt, I trust everything in the honeymoon suite was to your satisfaction?"

Everly blanched at the sound of Gregory's last name. She looked like she might vomit Dom Pérignon and canned cheese all over the Plaza's sleek marble floor.

"It was fine, thank you," Henry said. Then he reached for her hand and squeezed it tight. If pretending to be the jackass would spare her any embarrassment, he was happy to do it. "We'll be checking out now, and we're in a bit of a hurry, I'm afraid."

He needed to get Everly out of here, even if it meant they had to part ways. Clearly she wasn't up to chatting about her nonwedding with random strangers.

"Excellent. There are taxis right out front if you need one." The manager waved a hand toward the red carpeted valet area, where a shiny yellow cab sat waiting. "I'll just charge your stay to the card on file if that works, Mr. Hoyt?"

Gregory's credit card? Abso-freaking-lutely.

Henry shot the manager a smile. They should've charged more extras to the room. Every single dish on the room service menu, maybe. At minimum, they should've kept the robes. "Perfect."

He squeezed Everly's hand again, and this time, she squeezed his back—so hard that he got a cramp between his thumb and pointer finger, but he didn't dare let go.

Then everything seemed to move in slow motion as the valet opened the back door of the taxi, and Everly gave the uniformed attendant the address of her apartment on the Upper West Side. She dropped Henry's hand to gather layer upon layer of floaty tulle in an attempt to stuff her Cinderella gown into the cab's back seat.

Henry's jaw clenched. He wasn't ready to say goodbye. Not yet. They still had so much to talk about, so much to say to each other. Was he really going to just let her go with a wave, right here in front of the Plaza for all of Manhattan to see?

The thought of leaving for Bora-Bora without a proper goodbye seemed wholly surreal. He never felt like this before leaving on a trip. Usually, he couldn't wait to get on a plane and see where his next adventure would take him.

He raked a hand through his hair and bent to peer inside the back of the car. Everly looked impossibly small surrounded by all that gossamer fabric, like a delicate bridal figurine atop a wedding cake piled high with frothy swags of frosting.

She should be married right now. Henry's gut churned. He felt like an imposter all of a sudden, like he was standing in another man's shoes.

"Give us a minute?" he said to the driver through the open door.

The driver nodded and stepped out of the car as Henry climbed into the back seat to sit beside Everly.

"What are you doing?" she asked, casting him an amused glance as he batted a wisp of tulle from his face.

He shrugged one shoulder. "I just wanted to say goodbye before I left."

Henry was always saying goodbye. He should've been an expert at it by now.

Everly nodded, smile fading. "Goodbye," she said quietly, and there was an unmistakable hitch in her voice.

It was the hitch that did it—that subtle hint of the vulnerability swimming beneath the surface of the best friend act they were both trying to put on. Henry suddenly didn't want to pretend anymore. Couldn't, even if he tried.

He cupped her face, and the instant his fingertips made contact with her cheek, she closed her eyes and leaned into his touch. Henry would've sold his soul to stop time. To slow this impossible goodbye…maybe even stop it altogether.

"Come with me," he said again, dead serious this time.

"Henry, I can't." She shook her head, eyes swimming behind a veil of tears.

Her watery smile nearly killed him. It had been bad enough seeing her cry last night, but now…now he thought he might have something to do with those tears, and the last thing he'd ever want to do was make Everly cry. "I'm sorry."

Henry pressed his forehead to hers and slid his hand to the back of her neck. Her dark hair was silk against his fingertips. "Don't be sorry."

I'm not.

He wasn't sorry about a damn thing. Perhaps he should be, but he wasn't.

"Friends forever, right?" she whispered, but her eyes said something else. Something...more.

And then they were kissing again. Kissing like there was no tomorrow. Kissing like they'd just woken up together in the honeymoon suite. Kissing like neither one of them had ever uttered the word *mistake*.

Henry wasn't sure which one of them had started it this time, and he didn't care. All he knew was that he felt like at last he could breathe again. Breathe... feel...*live*.

Wasn't that what his father had always been urging him to do? *Live, son. Live as boldly and fully as possible. Do it while you can.*

Henry had never felt quite as alive as he did when he was kissing Everly. Last night, he'd almost been ready to chalk it up to novelty or the fulfillment of a lifelong fantasy he was almost too ashamed to acknowledge. But here they were again, and it was perfect. So sweet and exquisite that it felt like wild honey was coursing through his veins.

She's your best friend, a small voice in the back of his head said. *Are you* trying *to mess things up again?*

With no small amount of effort, he ended the kiss, pulling back just far enough to murmur against her lips. "Friends forever."

And then he climbed out of the car while he still could. If he didn't let her go now, he just might hijack her cab and reroute it to JFK. The sun hadn't quite come up yet. They could be in Bora-Bora by twilight, sitting on the beach with their toes buried in the sand—him in his tuxedo, her in her wedding gown, pink satin sash floating in the salty ocean breeze.

The driver shot him a questioning glance, and Henry nodded as he rapped three times on the roof of the cab.

The car pulled away, slowly at first, then in true New York form shot onto Fifth Avenue with a squeal of its tires. In a blink, Everly's cab blended into a sea of yellow cars, each one indistinguishable from the next. The sun rose over the horizon, bathing the surrounding buildings in molten gold. The dawn of a new day.

Friends forever. Henry's heart jerked in his chest, and he squinted against the blinding light. *Til death do us part.*

Chapter Three

Six weeks.

Six *weeks*.

Everly grabbed her cell phone, which she'd relegated to the farthest possible corner of her desk—desk Siberia, basically—and flipped it over to check the screen one more time before her late afternoon meeting with Colette.

Nothing. No notifications. No voice mails. No missed calls. Of course she'd known as much without checking the screen because she had all of her alerts set at full volume…just in case.

There'd been that brief trip to the photocopier a few minutes ago, though. She could have missed something.

Right, because waiting for the phone to ring for

the past six weeks hasn't honed your sense of hearing so much that you're practically a bat.

A bat, in regards to the fact that they have the best sense of hearing of all land mammals—not in a vampire sense. Although, Everly hadn't gotten much sleep in the past six weeks. She *did* sort of feel like the walking dead sometimes.

Wait, the walking dead meant zombies, didn't it? Not vampires. She was getting her monsters confused...or just generally losing her mind. One of the two, definitely.

"Oh, good grief," a voice said out of nowhere. "You're checking your phone again?"

Everly jumped, and her cell flew out of her hand, landing on the desk with a clatter. Every head in *Veil*'s open concept–style editorial department swiveled in her direction.

Everly's face went warm as she glanced up to find Daphne Ballantyne peering over the top of the cubicle divider that separated their work spaces.

Daphne arched a brow in the direction of Everly's phone. "Waiting for a call?"

"No, actually. I couldn't care less if anyone calls." Everly opened her top desk drawer, shoved the phone inside and then slammed the drawer closed to prove her point. Hopefully if it rang, she'd still be able to hear it. "I was just checking my Google Calendar to make sure I had the time right for my meeting with Colette."

"I see." Daphne's gaze flitted toward Everly's paper planner, where *Meeting with Colette 5:30* was written in bright blue sharpie and underlined in three bold strokes. "Totally believable."

Everly crossed her arms and sat back in her chair, cheeks now flaming with the heat of a thousand suns. "Did you need something, or were you just popping over to monitor my phone habits?"

Daphne winced. "Ouch. Since when do I need an actual reason to pop over?"

Since never. Everly loved having her desk so close to Daphne's. They typically chatted throughout the day, about anything from work-related matters to what color highlights Daphne should get in her tumbling blond hair. The latest—pastel pink. As the magazine's beauty editor, Daphne was constantly experimenting with her look. The cotton candy–hued highlights probably would have looked ridiculous on anyone else, but in true Daphne form, she rocked them. Right now, her hair was piled on top of her head in a relaxed ballerina bun anchored in place with nothing but a number two Ticonderoga pencil. Loose pink tendrils framed her heart-shaped face.

"Sorry." Everly sent Daphne a beseeching glance. "I didn't mean to snap. I'm just a little nervous about this meeting."

The email from Colette had hit Everly's inbox at nine o'clock last night, right as she was climbing into bed with a sheet mask on her face and her Netflix account tuned into something murdery. Her affection for rom-coms had cooled significantly six weeks ago.

A chill had immediately snaked its way up Everly's spine as she'd read Colette's message. It was a summons for all practical purposes. Her boss wanted to meet for an immediate "status update." Everly had been so worried about showing her face at *Veil* after getting dumped at the altar, but in the immediate aftermath, Colette had been surprisingly supportive. She hadn't uttered a word about the magazine's reputation—which was nothing short of shocking, considering that *Veil* was Colette Winter's entire life.

Not to mention the fact that Colette didn't exactly have a warm and fuzzy reputation.

Everly knew better than to question her good fortune, though. She'd simply thrown herself right back into work after the wedding. Since she'd failed spectacularly in the romance department, she'd decided to become a workaholic. That plan had seemed to work out spectacularly for Colette, so why not? Addison too. At the tender age of twenty-nine, Everly's sister was already the front-runner to take over Colette's position when she retired. She'd worked her tail off to get there, and Everly was ready to take note and follow in her big sister's footsteps. *Career first.* That was her new mantra.

Careers couldn't break your heart. They couldn't walk out on you and leave you humiliated in front of the entire world. Nor could they suddenly drop dead, as Everly's father had done back in college. One day he'd been there, and the next, he was just...gone. It was like he'd simply vanished. Everly still felt like she might collapse to her knees when she thought about getting the phone call from her mother about his car accident. Back then, during her freshman year at Columbia, she'd definitely crumpled...

But Henry had been there to catch her, and they'd been best friends ever since. Having lost his own father just months before, he understood her loss in a way that no one else could.

At the thought of Henry, Everly's throat closed up tight. She wished he'd stop invading her subconscious like that. It happened a million times a day. Just one of the many hazards of having so much of your life intertwined with another person's.

"Everything is going to be fine," Daphne said with her trademark optimism. "And you know...if you want to talk to Gregory, you should just pick up the phone and call him yourself. In fact, maybe a little closure would be a good thing."

Gregory? Everly blinked. Daphne thought she'd been checking her phone every five minutes for the past month and a half to see if her *runaway groom* had tried to contact her?

Of course she did. What did Everly expect? She hadn't breathed a word to anyone about sleeping with Henry on her wedding night. Not a soul. If she *had* confided in anyone, Daphne and Addison would have obviously been right at the top of the list.

She wasn't sure why she'd kept it to herself. She and the *Veil* girls usually talked about everything. They were her literal family, in addition to her work family. One day, they planned on running this office with Addison at the helm when Colette finally stepped down. They never kept secrets from each other.

How could she possibly explain that night with Henry, though? Everly knew how it would no doubt look from the outside—like a desperate rebound or even that Henry had taken advantage of her, neither of which were true.

Everly wasn't worried about appearances. She knew she could explain it in a way that her friends would understand. She just didn't dare. Something about that night—and the memory of it—was sacred. More sacred than she wanted to acknowledge... even to herself.

"Does everyone think I've been secretly pining over Gregory this entire time?" Just when she thought she'd reached rock bottom, it turned out there were whole new depths of humiliation to experience. *Oh, joy.* "Do you and Addison think that?"

"No, of course not," Daphne said a little too adamantly.

"Because I assure you I'm not," Everly said. *I'm secretly pining over Henry Aston instead.*

Correction: she was *not* pining. She simply… missed him.

Which was precisely why sleeping with him had been a colossal mistake. The biggest one she'd ever made in her whole life—even bigger than almost marrying Gregory.

"Understood. We're just a little concerned about you, that's all. You haven't been to Martini Night in weeks." Daphne waggled her expertly groomed eyebrows. "Tonight is Thursday, you know."

Thursday, also known to Everly's *Veil* squad as Martini Night. Right around the corner from the magazine's sleek high-rise office building in Manhattan's Upper East Side—conveniently located in close proximity to both Bloomingdale's *and* Magnolia Bakery—their favorite bar was tucked into a nice spot on a residential street lined with gorgeous Beaux Arts–style townhomes with lovely iron fretwork and decorative molding. The bar was called Bloom, and the *Veil* squad had been regulars long enough that the owner had invented a special cocktail just for them. The "wedding cake martini" was some magical-tasting combination of whipped cream–flavored vodka, vanilla vodka and pineapple juice, with a sugared rim. There were probably a few other ingredients tossed in there, all of which mixed together to taste exactly like a slice of decadent bridal-white wedding cake.

"We don't have to get our usual," Daphne said. "If

it's too soon for anything wedding-themed, I mean. We could get cosmos or something."

Everly waved a hand. "Please. We can't go to Bloom and get anything but our signature drink."

"Whatever you want. We just miss having you there." Daphne shot her a grin. "So you'll come tonight?"

Everly had planned on going straight home after her meeting with Colette and sinking into a bubble bath. She'd just been so tired lately. Getting through each day seemed to take superhuman effort. But maybe it was time to get back into the swing of things socially. She'd sworn off romance—and anything *remotely resembling* romance—not friendships.

Everly nodded. "Sure."

"Yay!" Daphne clapped her hands, and the numerous charm bracelets on her wrists tinkled like church bells. "And seriously, don't worry about your meeting with Colette. Maybe you're going to get a promotion. You've been on fire lately with your column."

Everly tilted her head. "You think?"

"Absolutely. You're really not pulling any punches." Daphne winked. "I kind of love this sassy new version of you."

Sassy. Everly sat up a little straighter. She liked the sound of that. She'd been answering as many email inquiries as she could in her weekly online edition of Lovebirds for *Veil*'s digital site. Since the "wedding," she'd been doing her best to give her most heartfelt advice possible. No holds barred.

"A promotion is just the thing I need right now," Everly said.

"Then you better hurry and get in there." Daphne tipped her head in the direction of Colette's office. "It's five twenty-nine."

See? This was why Everly's phone belonged on top of her desk and not hidden away in a drawer. A reminder about her meeting was probably flashing on its tiny screen right now. And *possibly* a message from Henry.

Stop thinking about him. He's probably on a beach somewhere with a Piña Colada in his hand, writing another freelance travel article that will eventually get nominated for a Wolf Granger Award. You're the furthest thing from his mind.

Henry and Everly had never been the type of best friends who talked every single day. They could go weeks, or sometimes even months, without any communication at all and fall right back into step when Henry reappeared in Manhattan. If Everly really needed him, she knew she could call and he'd drop whatever he was doing to be there for her.

But things were so weird now. So different. Sleeping together had amplified the ordinarily comfortable silence between them until Everly didn't quite know what to think anymore. Or feel, for that matter.

You feel *nothing but friendly affection for Henry*

Aston, Everly told herself as she stood to make her way to Colette's office.

She very nearly believed it.

"Everly," Colette said without looking up from her desk before Everly had a chance to knock on the open door or otherwise announce her arrival. Sometimes it seemed like her boss was omniscient. "Please come in."

Everly took a seat in one of the pristine faux fur chairs opposite Colette at her cream-colored lacquered desk. The entire space was decorated in various shades of white—eggshell, Chantilly, pearl, chiffon, parchment and snow, with a heavy emphasis on delicate *bridal* white. Naturally.

"Thank you for meeting with me," Everly said, even though she still had no real idea what she was doing here.

Colette's gaze darted from the contact sheets spread all over her desk—proofs from the magazine's latest bridal fashion photoshoot—to meet Everly's head-on. Her signature chin-length bob hairstyle seemed extra blunt today. Ultra polished, as sharp as a razor.

Everly gulped.

"Everly, we need to talk about your column." Colette said with exaggerated calm. Somehow, it was more terrifying than screaming would have been. "I know you've been going through a difficult time, but the advice you've been giving out these past six weeks is completely unacceptable."

"Unacceptable?" Everly managed to squeak.

"Last week you told a bride-to-be that if her groom didn't have a preference about cake flavors, he wasn't 'emotionally invested' in their big day, and she should seriously consider calling off her engagement." Colette's eyebrows crept closer to her hairline.

"In retrospect, that might seem a bit harsh," Everly said.

Was it, though? Gregory hadn't cared a whit about their wedding cake. Perhaps his lack of opinion on buttercream had been a giant red flag.

"Yesterday you advised a bride to 'kick her fiancé to the curb' because he'd accidentally caught a glimpse of her wedding gown two weeks before the ceremony." Colette sighed. "Are you sensing a theme here?"

"I'm just trying to give sound advice," Everly said. Romance was a minefield. She was simply trying to protect her readers. Couldn't her boss see that?

No, apparently.

"I'm taking you off the column, effective immediately," Colette said.

Wait. *What?*

Everly shook her head so hard that her teeth rattled. "No. *No.* Please."

Her career was all she had left. All she wanted. What was she supposed to do without her column?

"Clearly you're working through some feelings

right now, which is completely understandable in light of recent events." Those events being Everly's heart cracking into a million pieces and then her subsequently jumping her best friend's bones.

His kissable, captivating bones...

Oh my gosh, stop. She was in the middle of getting demoted and somehow still thinking about Henry.

If he ever did manage to call her again, she vowed to let it go straight to voice mail. Everly couldn't function like this. She'd always cared about Henry. But this...this was too much. Too all-consuming. Too risky. Like a heartbreak waiting to happen.

"For now, I'm moving you back into the position of junior reporter," Colette said.

Junior reporter, not even a senior one. This was almost as humiliating as being left at the altar.

"For how long?" Everly asked, blinking back tears.

"We can reassess in six months. In the meantime, try and give yourself a chance to heal." Colette smiled, which was truly terrifying. She was normally as stony-faced as the gargoyles on the old church on Lexington Avenue. "We're *Veil*. All brides want to hear from Lovebirds is that their fiancés love them unconditionally. You understand that, don't you?"

Everly's stomach cramped, and the back of her neck went hot. She felt like she might be sick. She understood all about the need for unconditional love—the yearning to love and be loved without fear of everything falling apart. Everly understood that feeling more than Colette could possibly know.

It was simply a risk she was unwilling, *unable*, to take. Not anymore.

An hour later, Everly sat perched at a high-top table at Bloom with her wedding cake martini in front of her, untouched. Stomach still in knots from the meeting with Colette, she couldn't bear to take a sip.

"Junior reporter." Addison scrunched her face. "I'm so sorry, Sis. I had no idea. If I had, you know I would've given you a heads up."

"I know you would." Everly nodded at her sister. Even after a ten-hour day at the office, Addison's shoulder-length chestnut waves looked artfully arranged. Her red Chanel lipstick perfectly smudge-free. With literal drawers full of padded headbands and a closet overflowing with tailored blazers, polka-dot blouses and LBDs, Addison had the sophisticated French girl aesthetic down pat. She hadn't inherited the role from Colette quite yet, but she already looked the part of editor-in-chief.

"Maybe this is a good thing," Daphne said, nodding encouragingly as she sipped from her crystal martini glass. "Maintaining a regular column like Lovebirds is stressful. You could use a break, Everly. After what you've been through, it's perfectly normal to need a little time to reassess."

The last thing Everly wanted was more time on her hands, though. Empty minutes were *not* her friend. When she wasn't busy working, her mind tended to wander into forbidden territory. Heck, even when she was busy writing something for the magazine, she still managed to check her phone every five minutes.

"I don't need time. I'm over it," Everly said. She picked up her drink, but the smell of the whipped cream vodka made her stomach churn. So she licked a tiny bit of sugar from the rim and put the drink back down without taking a sip.

Daphne and Addison exchanged a glance.

"What?" Everly demanded.

"It's just that it doesn't seem like you're completely over Gregory, hon." Daphne reached to give Everly's hand a squeeze. "And that's okay. Anyone in your position would be having a hard time right now."

Everly couldn't help but wonder how many other brides ended up in her position—that position being sleeping with their best friend the night they were supposed to get married. It couldn't be a high number.

"Daphne is right. I know you're trying your best, but you've definitely been distracted." Addison kindly dropped her gaze to her martini and didn't mention the ginormous typo she'd found in Everly's last column before it got uploaded to the *Veil* digital site.

Everly had somehow managed to convince herself that typing *dreaded kiss* in place of *wedded bliss* was an innocent mistake. Perhaps it had been more of a Freudian slip than she wanted to admit.

"And don't take this the wrong way, but you look exhausted," Daphne said. "I told you we've been worried about you."

Everly bit her lip. She suddenly remembered that Daphne had found her with her head on her desk the other day, sound asleep, at three o'clock in the afternoon. She thought about trying for a sip of her drink again but yawned instead.

Ron, the bartender, stopped by their table, interrupting the makeshift intervention that seemed to be happening. He pointed at the empty glasses in front of Addison and Daphne. "Another round, ladies?"

"Yes, please," Addison said.

Daphne grinned. "Thanks, Ron. You always take such good care of us."

"What about you, Everly?" Ron asked, then his gaze landed on her full glass. "Oh, wait. Is everything okay with your drink? You've barely touched it."

"It's fine. No worries. I guess I'm just not that thirsty tonight," Everly said. A wave of nausea washed over her at the smell coming from her martini. "You don't happen to have any crackers do you? Maybe some saltines or something?"

"For you?" Ron winked. "We sure do. I'll bring you a Coke, too. How does that sound?"

That sounded…perfect, actually. Saltines and a Coke, just like when she had the stomach flu as a little kid. Comfort food at its finest. If only she had a can of squirt cheese to go along with it.

"Crackers?" Addison narrowed her gaze at Everly as soon as Ron left.

Daphne tilted her head. "Naps at your desk?"

"Brain fog?" Addison added, because this list of Everly's current faults was such a fun group activity, apparently.

Everly attempted a subject change by pushing her martini toward the middle of the table. "Have these always been so strong? I can smell the alcohol a mile away."

Daphne gasped. "Oh. My. Gosh."

Addison's eyes went wide.

"What's with you two?" Everly asked. Honestly, a simple yes or no would have sufficed.

"Everly," Daphne said. Then she shook her head, as if what she were about to say was the most preposterous thing in the world. "You're not…"

Secretly in love with my best friend? Everly swallowed. *Don't say it. Please don't.*

She should've known better than to try and keep a secret from the *Veil* girls. Addison had always been able to read her like a book. She wasn't ready to rehash her wedding night. Not yet. And besides, she wasn't in *love* with Henry. She couldn't be. She wouldn't let herself be in love with him. She just sort of secretly wanted to sleep with him again. A lot more times.

Oh, good grief. What was *wrong* with her?

"Not what?" Everly said, feigning innocence as best she could.

Where were those saltines? This conversation was making her so nervous that her stomach was doing backflips.

"I think Daphne is trying to ask if you might be—" Addison leaned closer and whispered "—*pregnant*?"

Then Addison laughed, as if she'd meant the question in jest, but the laughter didn't quite meet her gaze.

Silence fell over their cozy little high-top. Ron dropped off the saltines, and Everly tried to thank him, but she couldn't seem to form the words.

Pregnant?

No, that was impossible. She and Gregory hadn't been intimate in months—the big fat warning sign that Everly had so naively overlooked in the lead-up to the ceremony.

But what about Henry? a tiny voice in the back of her head whispered.

No, absolutely not. She couldn't be pregnant with Henry's baby. She just couldn't. He was her *friend*. Things were already weird enough between them without adding a child to the mix. Besides, Everly was on birth control pills. It just wasn't possible.

Except she couldn't remember taking her pill the night of the wedding. Things had been so topsy-turvy. She clearly hadn't been thinking straight. And it might have been possible that she'd missed another dose in the week or two before the wedding. There'd been so much on her mind, and honestly, birth control didn't seem all too important when you weren't even sleeping with your fiancé.

She felt like she couldn't breathe all of a sudden. Visions of that night in the honeymoon suite flashed before her eyes like a dreamy, Impressionist painting—so soft, so breathtakingly sweet and yet, at the same time, so beautifully chaotic that it wasn't altogether discernible from up close. A tangled, radiant mess that only became clear from a distance. From hindsight.

Six weeks. Everly closed her eyes, squeezed them shut tight. *Six weeks.*

She'd been so wrapped up in trying not to miss Henry…trying to convince herself that it had all been a crazy mistake, and if they only tried hard enough, it would truly be like that night had never actually happened. She hadn't even noticed the signs.

Oh, Henry. Just forming his name in her thoughts felt like pressing a tender bruise. A lingering, exquisite ache. *What now?*

Chapter Four

How can we be sure this is accurate?" The plastic stick from the pregnancy test shook in Everly's hand as a second pink line appeared. Not a barely there blush pink, like the new line of bridal gowns from Monique Lhuillier, or a sweet carnation pink, like the highlights in Daphne's hair. Not even a cheery bubblegum pink, but a deep, vivid fuchsia. *Hot pink.* A pink too bold, too brazen to ignore. "Pregnancy tests sometimes give you false positive results, right?"

Addison nodded. "True. Although…"

"You just took four tests in a row and they're *all* positive, hon." Daphne nodded toward the bathroom sink, filled to overflowing with the debris from the four-pack of pregnancy tests they'd picked up at a drugstore immediately after leaving Bloom. "You're way pregnant."

With Henry's baby.

Everly felt like she was stuck in some alternate universe or one of those movies where time split into two different versions. Somehow she'd gotten stuck in the fantastical plot where she'd gotten dumped at the altar and ended up pregnant with her globetrotting best friend's baby instead of the version where really she belonged—living a calm, uneventful life on the Upper West Side married to Gregory. Her safe, mildly boring fiancé.

Now that he was out of her life, she had to admit that she didn't really miss going with him to Newport every other weekend so he could hang out at his yacht club. For as long as she'd known him, that boat had *never even left the harbor*. It was just a glorified social club, as were all the Wall Street functions they attended as part of his job as an investment banker. Gregory lived for those cocktail parties, but not once had he darkened the door of Bloom, even though she'd invited him to Martini Night numerous times.

She'd dodged a bullet. Everly knew that now. It had been a painful realization, but Gregory's dullness—his strict adherence to a daily routine—was precisely what had attracted her to him to begin with. He was predictable...dependable...*safe*.

Until he wasn't.

"Everly, are you okay? Talk to us. What's going

through your mind right now?" Addison rested a hand on Everly's shoulder.

"I was just thinking about how dull Gregory is," Everly said.

How had she failed to realize that before? The only truly interesting or surprising thing he'd ever done was make a jilted bride out of her.

Addison bit back a smile. "Sorry, I don't mean to laugh. That's just the absolute last thing I expected you to say right now."

"Why didn't either of you ever say anything? Surely you noticed." Everly glanced back and forth between Addison and Daphne.

Addison bit her lip. "Um…"

"Of course we did," Daphne said.

A burst of laughter escaped Addison, and she clasped a hand over her mouth.

"What? You know we talked about it." Daphne shrugged. "But don't worry, Everly. I'm no scientist, but I'm fairly certain dullness isn't hereditary. Your baby is going to be as bright and loving and adventurous as you are."

Everly blinked. Then she shook her head. That's right—they still thought the baby was Gregory's.

"The baby is going to be a lot more adventurous than you can possibly imagine." Everly snorted as she plunked herself down on the closed toilet and dropped her head in her hands.

Was this what hysteria felt like? For the second

time in as many months, the rug had been ripped completely out from under her life. Granted, she'd had more of an active role in this most recent upheaval. Still…

She was having some trouble wrapping her mind around it. Even through the fog of surprise, a part of her warmed instantly to the idea. She loved Henry with her whole heart. Always had. How could she not love the idea of a child with his kind eyes? His soft manner? His wild and wonderful heart?

Addison crossed her arms and peered down at her.

"I think she's in shock," she said to Daphne.

Daphne nodded. "I think you're right."

Everly sat back up and her head spun a little. She should have taken her saltines from Bloom to-go. She pressed a hand to her stomach.

A baby. She inhaled a ragged breath. *Like it or not, this changes everything.*

"There's something I need to tell you two," Everly said. "And it's going to be kind of a shocker."

No time like the present to let them know that she wouldn't be giving birth to a baby who came out of the womb in pressed khakis and a bland button-down shirt. She wanted to get that thought right out of their heads. Weirdly, the very idea of having a baby with Gregory seemed absurd, while being pregnant with Henry seemed almost…natural?

Sure, until you have to track him down on the

other side of the world to tell him he's going to be a dad.

One crisis at a time. Everly took a deep breath. She could do this. If Mindy Kaling could be a fabulous single career mom, so could she.

"More of a shock than the fact that you're pregnant?" Addison asked as she lowered herself until she was sitting down on the edge of the bathtub, meeting Everly's gaze.

Yes...no...maybe?

Before Everly could say anything, her cell phone rang and vibrated a little dance across the vanity where she'd placed it so she could properly time the results of the pregnancy test.

Everly glanced down at the notification on the screen and froze.

Henry Aston.

It was him...finally. Six weeks of complete and utter silence, and suddenly he calls, mere seconds after Everly finds out she's carrying his baby. Fate sure had an odd sense of humor sometimes.

A shock of sensation coursed through her, from the top of her head to the tips of her toes as she stared down at his name lighting up her iPhone. The intensity of it somehow felt like relief, hope, shock and fear all rolled into one.

Fear won out above all else. *I can't do this. Not now...not yet.*

She needed a plan first. She had to figure out how

to properly guard her heart before she told Henry he was going to be a father. Just because they were having a baby together didn't mean she could just let herself fall in love with him. On the contrary, it was all the more reason to stay on very friendly, very *safe* terms. Their friendship needed to remain intact more than ever now that they were going to be parents. She couldn't have a relationship with him when just a month and a half ago, she'd been walking down the aisle toward someone else. What would happen if they tried and she ended up alone…again? They'd be tied together for life, and seeing him all the time without being his friend would kill her. She couldn't do it. She'd rather have Henry's friendship than none of him at all.

Not to mention the fact that he hadn't said a word about wanting anything more. Granted, she hadn't given him much of a chance. But waking up beside him had terrified her to her core. She was afraid to want more. She couldn't let herself.

They'd both agreed. Their night together had been a mistake, and they were friends again now. They'd even sealed it with a kiss.

Everly pressed her fingertips to her lips as the memory of that kiss came back to her—the warmth of Henry's mouth moving against hers, the tender way he'd cradled her face in his hands, the urge she'd had to grab hold of the silk lapels of his tuxedo jacket and never let go. For a nonsensical second, she'd almost agreed to go with him to Bora-Bora, despite her complete and total inability to locate it on a map. That kiss hadn't been a friendly peck—it had been something else entirely. A vow…or perhaps a good-bye. Everly wasn't sure anymore.

She wasn't sure of anything. In the span of six weeks, her life had become utterly unrecognizable.

"Everly, do you need to answer that?" Daphne nodded at the phone, still blaring Henry's special ringtone—*I've Been Everywhere* by Johnny Cash.

Everly's stomach roiled.

Addison leaned over, glance at the phone and rolled her eyes. "It's nothing urgent." She pressed decline and ended the call. "Only Henry."

Everly's vision blurred, and she blinked as hard as she could, but she couldn't stop the tears from slipping quietly down her cheeks. She ran her hand over her belly, over the new life they'd created—the baby she already loved, sight unseen.

Only Henry…

What a spectacular mess she'd made of things.

"Sir, it's time to put your phone on airplane mode," the flight attendant said, smiling down at Henry in a stiff way that said she meant business.

"Sorry." He powered down his cell while she stood watching.

His disappointment in failing to reach Everly must

have been written all over his face, because the flight attendant lingered for a moment.

"We'll be at our destination by morning, if it makes you feel any better." She tilted her head, much friendlier now that he'd shown himself to be a good and decent passenger.

Henry always respected the rules of air travel and didn't much like passengers who caused trouble for the flight attendants. But he'd been trying to reach Everly for the past twelve hours, and his calls kept rolling to voice mail.

"A little." Henry held his thumb and pointer finger a fraction of an inch apart. For all practical purposes, morning would be too late.

He should've tried her sooner. But he'd wanted to give her some time to process what had happened between them. Some much-needed space. Plus, Henry never had trouble getting ahold of Everly. It wasn't like her to go this long without returning his messages. Usually, she picked up his calls on the very first ring. They'd always been the sort of friends who could go weeks or months without speaking to each other and then pick up right where they left off. The trouble was that Henry wasn't altogether sure *where* they'd left off. He felt like he was about to embark on a trek around the world without the benefit of a map.

"Here." The flight attendant placed a plastic champagne flute on the armrest of his business-class seat. "Maybe this will help you sleep."

With a pang in his chest, Henry watched the bubbles dance inside the fizzy liquid. The last time he'd had champagne, he'd been with Everly.

On her wedding night! his subconscious screamed. As if he could forget.

"No, thank you." He returned the drink to the flight attendant. "I'm good."

"Very well. Just let me know if you need anything," she said, and as she walked toward the bulkhead, the plane began crawling away from the gate.

Henry closed his eyes and waited for sleep to come. He never had trouble getting shut-eye on a plane. Or a train or any other form of transportation, for that matter. He'd once slept sitting straight up on an open-air bus while he shared a seat with a goat traveling from Kanpur to Dhanbad, no champagne necessary.

Besides, he didn't want even a hint of a hangover when he landed. A clear head would definitely be in order.

He should've called Everly sooner. Not a day had passed by in Bora-Bora when he hadn't wanted to hear her voice. Everywhere he looked, he imagined them there together—limbs entwined in the canopy bed in his hotel suite, walking hand in hand on the white-sand beaches, Everly's graceful form moving through the crystal blue waters with a ribbon of dark hair floating behind her.

She should've been there with him. He should've

insisted. Either that, or he should've stayed in Manhattan. The way they'd said goodbye that morning at the Plaza had just felt...wrong. And now six weeks had passed, and he had no idea where things stood between them.

Friends forever.

That's what they'd promised each other. Henry didn't want to screw that up. Couldn't. Everly was too important to him. She felt like the only family he had left. She'd needed space—space to *rebuild*, as she'd put it. And he'd needed these past six weeks to get the memory of their night together out of his system so that the next time he saw her, he'd be the old Henry. Everly's brotherly BFF. Her man of honor.

Whether or not the past month and a half had worked its magic remained to be seen.

Chapter Five

As much as Everly wanted to wallow in bed the following morning with a sleeve of crackers and a ginger ale, she didn't dare. Pregnant or not, she had a job to attend to. A career to save. If anything, the baby meant she needed to work harder than ever to get her column back. She had someone else to think about now, someone else to take care of—not just herself.

Colette had given her a timeline of six months. Everly needed to get back on her column even sooner, if possible. Once six months had come and gone, it would be hopeless. Shortly thereafter, she'd be off on maternity leave. How was she supposed to climb her way back up the corporate ladder when she wasn't even in the office?

One day at a time, she told herself as she twisted

her hair into an Audrey Hepburn–esque updo and secured it with a black velvet bow placed just behind her bangs. Today was the first Friday of the month, which meant the entire office would be meeting to discuss plans for the next print issue of *Veil*. The May pages had been put to bed a few days ago, so it was time to work on the most important edition of the entire year—the June issue.

September was traditionally the splashiest month for the mainstream fashion industry, but in the world of bridal fashion, June was the pinnacle. Bridal Fashion Week in New York always took place in April, which meant everyone in the office would be attending fashion shows in the coming weeks, choosing which gowns to showcase in their big June issue. The June edition also always featured a huge fifty-page spread on dream honeymoon destinations. Last year's June issue of *Veil* had been as thick as a brick.

Everly wasn't about to miss today's staff meeting. She intended to show up looking like a competent, polished professional ready to fight for a good story. She couldn't even remember what kind of assignments she'd been given back when she'd been a junior reporter the first time around. She shuddered to think of what she might get stuck with, so she brushed on an extra layer of mascara and slid into her nicest black shift dress. Givenchy…a passable imitation, at least. High-fashion armor.

"Wow, you look amazing." Addison stopped to

stare at Everly when she walked through the glass double doors of the *Veil* office. Fifteen minutes early, thank you very much. "Seriously. You're..."

Everly held up a hand. "Do not say *glowing*."

"Fine, I won't." Addison juggled her oversize Louis Vuitton bag, along with two paper cups decorated with pink cardboard coffee sleeves. "But for the record, you definitely are."

Everly gave one of her pearl earrings a nervous little twist. Glowing was nice. It was a *compliment*, for goodness' sake. She just hoped she wasn't glowing in a way that screamed, *Baby on board!*

Addison handed her one of the coffee cups as they walked side by side past the front desk and waved at the receptionist. "Here, Sis. I stopped by that coffee truck that we love down the street, and I got you your favorite—a vanilla cupcake latte. I thought you could use a little treat this morning." She winked. "It's decaf."

Everly plucked the cup from her hand. "Thank you. That was really thoughtful, but honestly, I'm fine."

Their steps slowed as they approached Everly's cubicle in the editorial department.

Addison lowered her voice. "It's okay to feel overwhelmed, you know. You've been through a lot lately. And now a baby...it's huge. *Wonderful*, obviously. Still, it's a lot to take on."

Everly inhaled a steadying breath. She was *not*

going to crumble this morning. She couldn't. "Truly, I'm good. I just want to treat today like it's any other day and focus on work."

"Whatever you want." Addison nodded. "Just remember I'm here for you. Daphne and I both are. I really wish you'd let us stay last night. I worry about you in that empty apartment, all on your own. Especially now."

Last year, when Everly and Addison's mother had decided to leave New York and move to Florida with her new husband, she'd left the girls the family apartment on 101st Street as their early inheritance. The apartment took up an entire floor of a converted townhome on one of the prettiest blocks between West End and Broadway, where the buildings were painted in soothing pastel shades and featured intricate ironwork and exterior columns. Sometimes Everly even thought their elaborate facades resembled frosting on a wedding cake.

With two large bedrooms and two bathrooms, the apartment was *sprawling* by Manhattan standards. Everly had imaged that she and Addison would share the space. Daphne too, possibly. But they'd both signed leases on places of their own already, so Everly had moved right in with the ghosts of her childhood. Then she'd gotten engaged to Gregory, and everyone assumed they'd live there together. Raise a family. Build a life. It was crazy what an engagement ring could make you believe.

"It's not totally empty," Everly countered. She hadn't been able to bring herself to purge the old family furniture in anticipation of Gregory moving in after the wedding. Maybe that was for the best. She'd definitely be redecorating now so she could turn the spare bedroom into a nursery.

Her heartbeat kicked up a notch, and she reminded herself to breathe. She needed to be thinking about work right now, not cribs and changing tables.

"Anyway, can we talk about something else, please?" Everly set her things down on her desk and smoothed down the front of her shift dress. "Like the staff meeting?"

"Sure, if that's what you want." Addison nodded. "Just don't forget that if you want moral support when you tell Gregory about the baby, you've got it."

God bless Everly's sister. Daphne too. After Henry's unexpected call last night, Everly had flipped her phone facedown and retreated into herself until she'd gone to bed. She hadn't even gotten around to telling Addison and Everly that Henry was the baby's father. It had just been too much to deal with all of a sudden. She'd been reeling—more so by his unexpected call than the fact that she was carrying the man's child. Which was ridiculous, but still. It was the truth.

And now Addison and Daphne still thought Gregory was the father. They were bringing her decaf vanilla cupcake lattes and treating her with kid gloves.

It was nice. *Really* nice. But it also made Everly feel like everyone thought she was on the brink of losing it, and they didn't even know the whole crazy truth.

Well, she wasn't going to lose it. Not today. Today, she was laser focused on things like lace gloves for fashion forward brides, wedding cakes frosted in ombré buttercream, and bridal stilettos with robin's egg–blue soles. She'd prove to Colette that nothing at all could steal her concentration. Not even her baby, and definitely not the baby's father, considering he was a world away right now, probably drinking out of a coconut or sleeping in a hammock by the beach.

You're going to have to deal with Henry at some point.

She had six missed call notifications from him last night and half as many voice mails, none of which she'd managed to bring herself to listen to. For once, she was grateful for the miles between them. The distance, along with the hefty difference in their time zones, gave her a little breathing room. But of course Everly was going to tell him about the baby…

Just as soon as she figured out how.

"I really want to snag a good assignment for the June issue." Everly squared her shoulders. "If there's any way you feel like you could back me up in the staff meeting, I'd really appreciate it. I promise I won't mess it up."

"I know you won't." Addison flashed her a wink. "I've got your back, Sis."

"What's all the whispering about over here?" Daphne said as she sashayed toward them in a frothy tulle dress that looked suspiciously like a tutu. Something only Daphne could pull off with panache. Her eyes widened as she swept Everly up and down with her gaze. "Hon, look at you. You're—"

"Don't say it!" Addison and Everly both blurted in unison.

"—glowing."

Everly's gaze narrowed. "You said it."

Daphne shrugged. "Sorry, I call it as I see it. You look amazing. Very Holly Golightly."

If Holly Golightly was secretly pregnant with Henry Aston's baby, Everly thought. She grabbed the latte and downed a third of it in one swallow.

Thankfully, no one else told her she was glowing in the hour that remained before the staff meeting. No one paid much attention to her at all, actually. Everly had the feeling the other writers didn't want to get too close to her, lest any of her bad career vibes rubbed off on them.

Fine. She'd show them.

She gathered her notepad and her heavily annotated copy of last year's June issue, which she'd been busy flagging with sticky notes all morning. Her mind was spinning with new ideas—elegant over-the-top gowns for brides over forty, *Emily in Paris*-inspired wedding dresses and maybe even a photo shoot on the banks of the Seine. Or perhaps

an entire article on the new crop of British designers specializing in pink gowns, accompanied by a
pictorial shot at the best pink travel spots in London,
like Peggy Porschen, EL&N Café or Pottery Lane in
Notting Hill. It felt good to be walking into a meeting fully prepared. She really hadn't been herself the
past six weeks. Everly had been so distracted with...
things...that she hadn't noticed what a fog she'd been
in at work. Losing her column had been a massive
wake-up call.

Daphne waved Everly over toward the corner
where she stood alongside a few of the other department editors as she walked into the conference room.
Everly bypassed "writers row," where she usually
sat with the other columnists and senior writers at
the sleek glass conference table, and planted herself
beside Daphne, grateful for the change in scenery.

As always, Colette swept into the room and kicked
off the meeting a full ten minutes earlier than its
scheduled time.

"Good morning, everyone," she said, glossy blunt
bob shining under the fluorescent office lights as she
took her place at the head of the table. "Welcome to
the most important time of the year here at *Veil*, as
we begin preparations for the legendary June issue.
It's nice to see everyone looking so eager and prepared."

Everly stood up a little straighter. Was she imagining things, or had Colette's gaze flitted in her di-

rection as she'd said those last few words? Things were looking up already. *Thank goodness*.

"Before we get started brainstorming feature articles and the like, I have a very special announcement to make about this edition." Colette leaned forward and planted her hands on the table in what could only be described as a power pose. "As you know, the June issue is fashion-centric, but we always include a special pull-out fifty-page honeymoon feature. We've had unprecedented advertising interest in the honeymoon section this year, so we've decided to do something different. *Extra*-special."

Colette's eyes glittered, and Everly couldn't help but wonder what on earth she had up her couture sleeve. She glanced at Addison, positioned immediately to Colette's left, but her expression was as curious as all the other higher-ups seated around the table. Then Everly's gaze shifted to Colette's right, where the chair closest to her sat empty.

Weird. She couldn't figure out which staff member wasn't in attendance. Everyone seemed to be there.

"For this year's June issue, we're expanding the honeymoon travel highlight to an unprecedented seventy-five pages," Colette announced. "We're expanding the regular fashion and general wedding section by an additional fifty pages, as well."

Someone standing behind Everly let out a low whistle. It was no wonder. These updated page counts, along with additional ads, meant the issue would be over four hundred pages long. That was *a lot* of wedded bliss.

It was also a lot of work. The editorial staff was stretched so thin this time of year that Addison usually worked twelve-hour days until the June issue was complete.

Everly glanced at her sister. Sure enough, her face was etched with concern.

"Not to worry, though. We're bringing on a guest editor specifically to put together the honeymoon special." Colette smiled bigger and brighter than Everly had ever witnessed before. "This has been in the works for a while now, and I'm delighted we've managed to keep the news secret for this long. A press release will be going out later today, but for now, you're all the first to know that our June honeymoon travel feature will be guest edited by none other than five-time Wolf Granger nominee and all-around adventurer..."

Time came to a standstill all of a sudden. Everly became hyperaware of the sound of her own breathing. Her heartbeat pounded impossibly loud in her ears.

Five-time Wolf Granger nominee? The Wolf Granger Award was the equivalent of a Pulitzer in the world of adventure and travel writing. Henry had been nominated several years in a row...

Five, in fact.

No. Everly was going to faint. She was going to slink to the ground and lose consciousness right there on the conference room floor in an elegant pile of faux Givenchy. *It's not him. It can't be.*

Henry wouldn't keep this kind of thing from her. He would've given her some sort of warning before popping up as a guest editor at her magazine. In all their years of friendship, they'd never kept secrets from each other.

Think again. Aren't you keeping a very important secret from him right now? *Pot, meet kettle.*

Time started moving again—slowly, like in a dream. Colette was still talking, but Everly couldn't make sense of anything she said because her thoughts had snagged on a moment during the excruciating elevator ride she'd shared with Henry the morning after her wedding. He'd met her gaze in the elevator mirror, and she'd been so worried that he was about to express his regrets about the night before that she'd wanted to clamp her hands over her ears.

E, there's something I need to tell you...it's not about last night.

She'd been in such a hurry to get out of that fancy hotel and pretend nothing about the prior twenty-four hours had been real that she hadn't let him finish. She'd all but raced him to the taxi stand. Then he'd kissed her, and she'd forgotten every single reason why she'd wanted so badly to flee.

Everly wobbled on her stilettos. So *this* was why

he'd been trying to get in touch with her last night. The one time she'd dodged his calls, he'd been trying to tell her that they were about to be coworkers!

"Please help me welcome our new guest editor, the esteemed Henry Aston," Colette said.

The room burst into applause, snapping Everly out of her trance and catapulting her back to the unbearable present, in which Henry was striding into the conference room looking like he'd just walked off the cover *GQ Magazine*. He was wearing an impeccably cut suit and the Hermès tie that Everly had helped him pick out for the Wolf Granger Awards two years ago. She herself had fashioned it into a perfect Windsor knot for him before accompanying him to the ceremony at the Natural History Museum in London. As friends…

Obviously.

Henry shook hands with Colette, then turned his attention to the rest of the room. His gaze found hers in an instant, and as he started to address the staff, Everly's arms went limp at her sides. The annotated copy of last year's June edition—the one she'd so carefully studied in preparation for this very meeting—fluttered to the floor, followed by her notepad. Everly heard someone gasp and, with a sinking feeling, realized it was her.

Then the whole world went dark.

"Thank you for the warm welcome, Colette. I'm happy to be here at *Veil*—" Henry couldn't look away from Everly. He hoped the word salad coming out of his mouth made sense, because all he could do was stare, transfixed. She looked more beautiful than he'd ever seen her—even more lovely than her wedding night. Maybe it was simply his imagination, but she was radiant. Luminous, even as she glared at him with a terrible combination of shock and fury in her violet eyes that made Henry feel like he'd been sucker punched.

Obviously, she hadn't listened to his numerous voice mails from last night. His presence had clearly caught Everly off guard, and from the looks of things, she was less than thrilled to see him.

This is what happens when you venture out of the friend zone. There's no going back.

"Ah…" Henry stumbled over his words, cleared his throat as he averted his gaze from Everly and tried again. "It's an honor to guest edit the legendary June issue, and I have no doubt—"

A thud echoed through the conference room, accompanied by a flurry of pages, cutting him off. Henry's head snapped back toward Everly just in time to see her eyelashes flutter as she went boneless and slid slowly to the floor.

Henry was at her side in a flash. He wasn't sure how he did it exactly. For all he knew, he could have hurdled over the conference table. He just knew he needed to get to her before she hit her head or otherwise injured herself. The next few seconds were a blur of confusion as everyone tried to figure out what just happened. Luckily, Daphne realized what was going on after the magazine hit the floor and managed to break Everly's fall. Henry got there just in time to cradle Everly's head in his hands before she banged it on the ground.

Addison was only a split second behind. "Oh my gosh. Everly? *Everly.* Are you okay?"

Henry gave Everly's cheek a gentle pat, trying to wake her. He'd somehow ended up sprawled on the floor with her head in his lap.

Addison's gaze flew toward Daphne. "Did you see what happened?"

"I think she, um, *fainted*," Daphne said, seeming to place special emphasis on that last word.

Henry was flummoxed. He'd never known Everly to faint before. He glanced up at Addison and Daphne, who seemed to be locked into some sort of silent communication. "Something must be really wrong. Has she been sick?"

Colette clapped her hands, bringing the buzz of conversation in the room to an immediate halt. "Meeting adjourned, everyone. We'll regroup later. Let's clear the room and give Everly some space."

"Someone needs to call 911," Henry snapped. *"Now."*

Addison darted to the table to grab her phone as the rest of the staff, minus Henry and Daphne, filed out of the room. Just as the 911 operator came on the line, Everly stirred.

"Hey there, Sleeping Beauty," Henry said, as her eyes fluttered open and her gaze locked with his. Something in his chest loosened at the sight of her, conscious again. He took a deep, desperate gulp of air.

"Henry," she said, and for a second, her face split into a glorious smile. Henry could have wept with relief. Then that giddy grin vanished as quickly as it had appeared.

Everly scrambled to a sitting position and backed away, just out of reach. "What are you doing here? And what happened? Why am I on the *conference room floor?*"

"You fainted," Daphne said as she crouched to wrap an arm around Everly's shoulders.

"Fainted?" Everly echoed.

"Yes." Addison ended her call and came to kneel on Everly's other side. "The paramedics are on their way."

Henry felt like the odd man out all of a sudden. No one seemed to be looking directly at him.

Just how badly had he damaged their friendship? Panic clawed at his insides. And yet, if he could have lived that night at the Plaza over again, he wasn't entirely sure he would've done things differently. He still couldn't bring himself to call making love with Everly a mistake.

"You gave us all a real scare." He swallowed, and then a sense of calm washed over him as his gaze landed on the delicate silver E charm resting in the dip between her collarbones. She'd ditched the huge diamond pendant Gregory had given her and gone back to wearing the simple silver charm from Henry. It probably wasn't significant. Why would she want to continue wearing a gift from the man who'd walked out on her in the middle of their wedding?

Still, seeing her wearing it again was a balm to his soul. Maybe things between them weren't as messed up as they'd seemed.

"Are you feeling okay?" Henry asked, reaching for her hand and squeezing it tight.

"I'm fine." She sat up a little straighter but, to his great relief, didn't let go. Instead, she wound her fingers through his, almost like old times. "I'm just…"

She glanced at Daphne and Addison.

"Actually, she's…" Addison started.

"*Fine*," Everly interjected, loudly enough to peel the paint off the walls. "Hunky-dory. I think I just locked my knees or something."

"Totally." Daphne cleared her throat and muttered something that sounded an awful lot like *or something*.

Locked her knees?

Henry shook his head. He couldn't understand why Daphne and Addison didn't seem as alarmed as he was. "I really think you should let EMS check you out, just in case."

No sooner had the words left Henry's mouth than

Colette ushered three uniformed paramedics through the double glass doors of the conference room.

"She's right in here," Colette said. Relief etched her features as her gaze swept over Everly. "Oh, thank goodness. You're awake. How are you feeling?"

"I'm great." Everly smiled, but her face was still alarmingly pale. "Ready to restart the meeting. I have a list of ideas, and—"

"Everly, honey." Colette shook her head. "I think we just need to concentrate on your health right now. I have the perfect writing assignment for you. Something nice and low stress. We can discuss it when you feel better."

Everly struggled to scramble to her feet. "Colette, please. I—"

"Sit back down," Henry said, a fair bit sharper than he'd intended. He couldn't help it. Watching her lose consciousness like that had shaken him to his core.

Everly flinched, and then her expression went icy. "Excuse me? I wasn't speaking to you, Henry. This is between Colette and me."

Henry's jaw clenched.

She was angry at him. Fine, he probably deserved it. But a minute ago she'd been unconscious with her head in his lap, so Henry wasn't about to let her just get up and go back to work like everything was normal—or, as Everly had put it, "hunky-dory."

"Henry is right, Everly." Colette crossed her arms.

"You and I can talk more about the June issue to-morrow. Once you've been checked over, I'd like you to go home and get some rest…assuming you don't need to be admitted to the hospital."

"The hospital? I'm certain that's not necessary." Everly tucked a stray lock of hair behind her ear as one of the paramedics strapped a blood pressure monitor around her arm.

"Could you sit quietly for a moment, please?" the paramedic said.

"Oh." Everly nodded. "Sure."

Addison spread her arms out wide and began herding everyone who wasn't dressed in an EMS uniform out of the room. "Let's go. I'm sure Everly is fine, but she might want a little privacy."

Henry's feet felt like lead. Things between them were clearly weird, but he didn't want to leave until he knew for certain she was okay. He cast Everly a beseeching look, but she was preoccupied whispering something to one of the paramedics.

"Henry?" Addison arched an eyebrow at him from the doorway. "Are you coming?"

He lingered for another second or two, waiting for Everly to tell him to stay, like the time during junior year at Columbia when she'd accidentally cut her finger picking up the pieces of a broken coffee cup and had to get stitches. She'd insisted he remain in the exam room with her at the health center while she got stitched up. So Henry had stayed. And he hadn't even flinched when she squeezed his bicep so hard with her free hand that she left behind little half-moon marks from her pretty pink manicured nails. It had taken all night for them to fade.

Everly didn't ask him to stay this time, though. This time...

She didn't so much as look at him.

Chapter Six

Everly trudged up the interior steps of the town-home, where her apartment occupied the entire third floor of the lilac-colored building, trying to imagine what it was going to be like maneuvering a stroller up these stairs…

Not the easiest thing in the world, perhaps. But at the moment, she would've preferred the baby stroller to the baggage she was currently dragging behind her—metaphorical baggage in the form of Addison and Henry, who'd both insisted on escorting her home from the office after her fainting spell.

"I promise I don't need a babysitter," she said as she turned the key in the lock and entered her apartment. "I'm going to do exactly as Colette ordered and get some rest before I go back to work tomorrow."

Despite her protests, Addison and Henry both followed her inside. Because of course they did.

Everly turned to face them both, careful to not meet Henry's gaze head-on. If she looked directly at him, he'd probably see how hurt she'd been by his sudden appearance at her office. Crushed, really.

Granted, if she'd picked up the phone last night when he'd called, she would've known to expect him. But she'd been in the middle of a life-changing, friendship-altering revelation of monumental proportions at the time. Drowning in pregnancy tests and little pink lines. And now, less than twenty-four hours after getting demoted, she'd ended up sprawled all over the floor of the *Veil* offices in front of the magazine's entire staff. So yeah, she was feeling a little fragile…tender…*vulnerable*.

Everly didn't want to feel like this when she told Henry about the pregnancy. She wanted to project an aura of competent single motherhood or, at the very least, seem like she wasn't coming apart at the seams. She didn't want to need Henry or, heaven forbid, accidentally fall in love with him. Loving someone inevitably meant losing them. At least that had been Everly's experience with every man she'd ever loved. Right now, she just really needed Henry to leave until she could practice her game face.

Didn't he have a magazine to edit, anyway?

"I can stay," Addison said, but her smartwatch was currently lighting up her wrist like a Christmas tree. She glanced down at it and pulled a face. "I just need to make a quick call first. Colette wants to go over the schedule for Bridal Fashion Week."

"Go, Addison. It's fine." Henry shot Everly one of his lopsided smiles, which made her go all gooey inside. Good grief, she wasn't going to faint again, was she? "I can stay."

Everly's face went warm. Why was it so unseasonably hot in her apartment all of a sudden? And why did Henry have to wear that Hermés tie? It made her wonder if he'd worn it intentionally—if he'd been thinking about her as he'd slipped it around the collar of the exquisite dress shirt he was wearing. Everly had never seen the shirt before. It screamed Savile Row and brought out the blue in his eyes in a way that made her forget how to breathe. Pinpoint Oxford—it had to be. She'd just woken up with her face in his lap, and the fabric had been ridiculously soft against her cheek. For a second there, she'd been so happy, so *elated*, to see him gazing down at her that she'd forgotten they were supposed to be just friends.

"Neither of you needs to stay," Everly reiterated.

What she needed was a snack, not round-the-clock surveillance. According to the paramedics, low blood sugar had likely been the culprit this morning, along with the new change in her hormones. Everly was going to have to get better about eating small meals throughout the day, which was definitely doable. She didn't think something that simple required a village.

"Addison? A little help here? Tell your sister she shouldn't be alone right now. Please." Henry scrubbed his face, and Everly looked at him. *Really* looked.

That's when she noticed tired lines around his eyes and the strain in the set of his jaw. He was either stressed or exhausted—probably both. Everly swallowed as a tiny dent pinged in the emotional armor she'd erected around herself.

Addison cast a pleading glance at her. "Ev, come on. We're just worried about you, that's all. What's with you anyway? You always jump at the chance to spend more time with Henry."

True…but that was then, and this was now. So much had changed.

"I'm sure Henry is jet-lagged." Everly swiveled her attention toward him and crossed her arms. A barrier, of sorts. "Have you even had a chance to stop by your apartment yet, or did you go straight to the office from the airport?"

Henry unbuttoned his suit jacket and sat down on the sofa, clearly intending to stay a while. "Actually, I won't be staying at my apartment while I'm here. I sold it last month."

The bottom dropped out of Everly's stomach. She might need to sit down. "Y-you mean you're leaving New York? *Permanently?*"

Granted, he was hardly ever here. When he wasn't traveling, he was mostly based at his flat in London since that's where the *Wanderlust* headquarters were

located. Still, giving up his Gramercy Park address
felt like a major change—a change that had nothing
whatsoever to do with Everly, but she felt a familiar pang of abandonment at the news, all the same.

Her father hadn't abandoned her. Intellectually,
Everly knew this. The loss had left her so untethered, though. So rudderless. Her mother had been a
mess in the wake of her father's accident. If it hadn't
been for Henry, Everly felt like she might've floated
away. When Gregory walked out on her in the middle of their wedding, that same untethered feeling
had come rushing back. No wonder she'd clung to
Henry like a lifeline.

And now he was leaving the country. For good.

Everly's bottom lip began to quiver. She bit down
hard on it and hoped he didn't notice.

"I've spent less than ten days there in the past
twenty-four months. The real estate market is boom-
ing, so it seemed like the right time to finally pull the
plug and let it go. It's more practical to stay in hotels
or private rentals when I'm in town," Henry said.

"Makes sense," Addison said, oblivious to the
swirl of panic gathering in Everly's chest. "If you
don't have an apartment here anymore, where are
you staying while you're here working for *Veil?*"

"The magazine is putting me up at the Carlyle. I'm
checking in later this evening." Henry loosened his
tie and leaned back against Everly's throw pillows.

He looked so at home here. It made Everly want

to curl up beside him and rest her head on his shoulder. Instead, she slid a smidge closer to the opposite end of the couch.

Addison's face lit up. "Why don't you stay here with Everly instead?"

Henry's gaze flew to Everly, and her heart leaped straight to her throat.

"I mean, unless you'd rather stay in luxurious splendor at the Carlyle." Addison laughed. "Everly's got plenty of space here, though. And you two would have plenty of time to hang out, especially now that Gregory is out of the picture."

Everly stared at sister, mouth agape. *Really? We're going there?*

Addison arched an eyebrow. "What? Just last night you were telling Daphne and me how terminally boring Gregory is. You're better off and you know it."

Henry released a snort of laughter and tried to cover it with a cough.

"Seriously, why don't you stay here, Henry? Even if just for the first couple nights?" Addison shot Everly a sympathetic smile. "Sis, we're all just worried about you. Even Colette, which is truly alarming. You know how she is. All she cares about is *Veil*. It's unusual for her to even think about anything but the magazine. Please just humor us and let Henry look after you for the next few days."

Addison pinned her with a look. She was obviously worried because of the pregnancy, but at least she'd realized that Everly hadn't had a chance to tell Henry about it. If Everly didn't acquiesce and let Henry stay, Addison might go rogue and spill the beans. When Addison went into girl boss mode, she was pretty unstoppable. And she was beginning to get that look about her.

Everly tried shooting her own look back at Addison—a look that said, *Spoiler alert: my lovable best friend Henry is actually the father of my baby.* But the message appeared to fly straight over her sister's head.

"How about it, E?" Henry said softly, with just a slight hint of hesitation in his voice, too subtle for anyone besides Everly to notice. Their night together had left its mark on him, too, and for the first time since Everly had known Henry, her lifeline seemed a little untethered himself.

Without quite realizing what she was doing, Everly toyed with the necklace at her throat. Her fingertips traced the shape of the E charm Henry had given her. The feel of the silver against her skin was comforting, like muscle memory—familiar and new at the same time. A piece of her heart had slipped back in place when she'd put it on this morning.

Henry's gaze dropped to the charm, and then he slowly lifted his eyes to hers and smiled. Everly had the crazy thought that she'd somehow summoned him back to her, just by the simple act of wearing the charm again. She knew it wasn't true, but the idea

that she could bring him home whenever she wanted
was such a lovely thought that she let herself believe.
Just for a moment.

"If you insist, then yes," she said, and her breath
caught on her answer. "You can stay."

As soon as Addison left to go back to the office,
Everly's apartment seemed to shrink by at least three
sizes. Henry almost felt like he was back in the bathroom of the Plaza's honeymoon suite, hemmed in by
Everly's diaphanous gown and nearly a decade of
suppressed longing.

Mostly the latter.

"I think I'll lie down for a little bit," Everly said
without fully meeting his gaze.

Henry hated that she didn't want to look at him
anymore. Every now and then, she seemed to forget
and let her guard down, and those moments felt as
natural and easy as breathing. But inevitably, she'd
catch herself and resume focusing on his forehead
or his left ear or some other random part of him in
close proximity to his eyes. She may as well have
been ignoring him entirely, though.

This huge, unspeakable thing—the night they'd
spent together, the awkward goodbye, all of it—was
a like a gauzy curtain that had fallen between them.
They could still see each other, but not clearly enough
to know what lay on the other side. Henry couldn't
help but think of the moment a groom lifted the veil

away from his bride's face and the rush of adrenaline that must surely come when he set eyes on her for the first time, ready to make promises to each other. To have and to hold. To love and to cherish. In sickness and in health.

He'd been working at *Veil* for less than a day and was already thinking in terms of wedding metaphors. This wasn't a good sign.

"A nap sounds like just what the doctor ordered," Henry said, as if speaking to a casual acquaintance. "Get some rest."

Everly nodded. "Make yourself at home. The guest room is all yours."

"Thanks," Henry said and shoved his hands in his trouser pockets as she disappeared into her bedroom and shut the door.

The guest room is all yours.

Ouch. He hadn't expected to share Everly's bed, but the fact that she'd felt the need to make certain he knew where he'd be sleeping hurt. He knew it shouldn't, but it did.

He took a deep breath and looked around. Everly's place hadn't changed a bit. The apartment was nice. Cozy, full of bookshelves and an oval-shaped space between the living area and the master bedroom that Everly used as a home office. Her rose-gold laptop sat on a writing desk that had once belonged to her father. The surrounding shelves held row upon row of back issues of *Veil*.

That one small space was the only place in the entire apartment that felt like Everly. The rest still looked almost exactly as it had back before she'd inherited it. Henry had never been able to imagine Gregory living here. Or maybe he just hadn't wanted to.

Enough. He raked a hand through his hair, banished all thoughts of Everly's erstwhile groom from his head and got on with more practical things. First he called the *Veil* offices and made arrangements for his bags to be delivered to the apartment. Then he shed his suit jacket, rolled up his sleeves and took a quick inventory of the kitchen. When Everly got up, she needed to eat. He wanted her to have something substantial, preferably home-cooked. Comfort food seemed to be in order after a fainting spell.

He grabbed a few eggs, some flour and an opened tub of shredded parmesan cheese he found at the back of the fridge. After connecting his phone to Everly's Bluetooth speaker, he put on an Italian dinner party-themed playlist and got to work. He mixed the dough with his hands, the old-fashioned way. Then he rolled it out and used the pasta setting on Everly's standing mixer to cut fine, thin layers of fettuccine. He'd just finished cleaning up the mess and getting everything plated when Everly stumbled out of her bedroom in an old Columbia T-shirt and yoga pants, glossy hair fashioned into a high ponytail.

"I can't believe I slept so long. What've you been

doing all afternoon? Have you been bored out of your mind?" She stopped short when she reached the kitchen and caught sight of Henry sprinkling a generous amount of parmesan cheese over a nest of freshly cooked pasta.

"I managed to keep myself busy," he said with a wink.

Color flooded her face. Pink, like cherry blossoms in springtime. "I can see that. What is all of this?"

"Cacio e pepe." He threw a dish towel over his shoulder, grabbed their plates and headed toward the dining room table. "I thought you might be hungry when you got up."

"But where did all of this come from?" Everly asked as she followed him.

He set the plates down on the table and pulled out a chair for her. "Sit. I'll light the candles."

She lowered herself into the chair and blinked up at him, as dazed as if she were still back in her bed dreaming. "Those look like the silver candlesticks my mom always used for Christmas dinner."

"I found them in one of your kitchen cabinets when I was looking for your rolling pin," Henry said as he struck a match and held it over a slim tapered candle.

"I have a rolling pin?" Everly grinned. The flames on the candles flickered to life, bathing her features in a soft golden glow.

Henry's heart turned over in his chest. He balled the matchbook in his fist. "Indeed you do."

"So you didn't order this?" She gaped at the pasta in front of her. "I don't recall having fettuccine noodles in the pantry."

"You didn't." Henry sat down beside her and spread his napkin in his lap.

"Henry Aston, are you telling me you just made me homemade pasta from scratch?" Everly's eyes danced, and finally...*finally*...things felt normal between them again.

Except for the way he ached with need every time he set eyes on her.

That was still very much a problem, but it was one that Henry was doing his level best to ignore.

"Don't be too impressed. *Cacio e pepe* literally translates to *cheese and pepper*." He twirled his fork into the nest of pasta on his plate. "This is basically glorified macaroni and cheese."

"We usually order a pizza, and you just sneakily made pasta from scratch while I was taking a nap. I'm definitely impressed." She took a bite, and her eyes nearly rolled back in her head. "Oh my gosh. This is the best thing I've ever tasted. You've been holding out on me. When did you learn how to throw together a meal like this?"

"Last summer when I was in Rome for *Wanderlust*. I did a story on cooking schools for travelers. Believe it or not, I can also make a mean tiramisu."

Everly shook her head and laughed as she twirled her fork. "Nope. No way. You're going to have to prove it to me."

"That's perfectly doable since I'm going to be staying here for the next four weeks," Henry said.

Everly's gaze dropped to her plate. "Four weeks is a long time. You're sure you wouldn't rather stay at the Carlyle after a night or two?"

"Absolutely." Henry nodded. He practically *lived* in hotels. "Listen, E. I'm sorry I waited until the last minute to try and tell you about the guest editing gig at *Veil*. I never intended to spring it on you like that."

"It's okay. You tried to tell me." She swallowed as she toyed with her pasta with her fork. "I remember. I just didn't give you a chance to get the words out."

A lot of things had gone unsaid that morning, and now it was too late. The only way to preserve their friendship was to plow ahead. Keep moving forward...

Henry would just have to get used to the fact that a part of his heart would always remain back in that room at the Plaza.

"I'd planned on telling you at the wedding reception. I wanted it to be a surprise." He blew out a breath. "Believe me, I realize now how presumptuous that sounds. It was supposed to be your day, not mine."

And in the end, it had turned out to be *theirs*. No amount of pretending could erase that.

"It's not presumptuous. I would've been thrilled with a surprise like that," she said, eyes dancing with candlelight.

Henry nodded, not quite trusting himself to speak. They were tiptoeing around the elephant in the room, and the more they talked, the more he felt like he was sharing a meal with his best friend Everly, the more he let his guard down. There was no telling what might accidentally fly out of his mouth.

"I just can't figure out why, though? You've never expressed any interest in working for *Veil. Wanderlust* loves you. Spending an entire month as a guest editor doesn't seem like you at all," Everly said.

Why had he accepted Colette's offer?

Because I felt like I was losing you, and agreeing to this gig was like trying to grab hold of our friendship with both hands.

The truth hit Henry right in the solar plexus. Deep down, he'd always known things between them would never be the same once she'd married Gregory. He just hadn't wanted to face reality until it had slapped him in the face in the form of Everly walking down the aisle in a wedding gown. In that single heart-stopping moment, he'd realized how much Everly meant to him…how much he loved her.

As a friend, of course.

Liar.

"Because of you, obviously," he said, and Everly's fork paused halfway to her mouth. "I thought it would be fun to work together. We haven't done that sort of thing since college. So when Colette reached out and asked if I'd edit the honeymoon special, I asked for a leave of absence from *Wanderlust*. They were happy to agree. I'm sure they think guest editing *Veil*'s famous June issue will be great PR for *Wanderlust*, too."

He swallowed. Technically, everything he'd said was the truth. He'd just wrung every last drop of emotion from the equation.

Everly sat back in her chair. "Well, I hate to tell you this, but I highly doubt we'll actually be working together. I've been demoted."

"Are you serious?" Henry sat his fork down. He'd suddenly lost his appetite. Surely this wasn't about the wedding. "Why?"

"Dead serious. Colette pulled me off my column yesterday. I'm a junior reporter now, and after today's fainting incident, I'll be lucky if she lets me write anything at all." She sighed. "Apparently, my column has lost its sense of romance. I let the cat out of the bag and started telling brides there's no such thing as unconditional love."

Numbness infused Henry's body. Since when had Everly decided not to believe in love? *Since spending the night with* you, *apparently.* "E, I know you don't believe that."

"Maybe I do." She lifted her chin in defiance, but her gaze went soft. Soft…and more than a little bit sad. "Or maybe I'm just tired of feeling like I'm not lovable enough or desirable enough for someone to stick around."

A tightness wound its way around Henry's chest that made it impossible breathe. Impossible to swallow. He should've been happy to have Everly opening up to him again, but he wasn't ready to hear this, wasn't ready to see the pain and loneliness shimmering in her wide violet eyes.

She's talking about her father, he told himself. Henry knew all too well how deeply her dad's death had affected her. Gregory's behavior on their wedding night had surely ripped the Band-Aid off that loss and brought everything back, especially after she'd implied that Gregory hadn't found her desirable…hadn't wanted her.

He rested his hand on the table and slid it toward hers until their fingertips were nearly touching. Invisible sparks zinged between them. So close…and yet the distance between their hands somehow felt like an endless divide.

"Not everyone leaves, E," Henry said quietly. *I'm here now, darling. I'm right here.*

Their gazes collided. Neither of them took a breath, and just like that, they were dancing in that dangerous place between friendship and something more. Henry could practically feel her in his arms, surrendering to the feelings that they were both trying so hard to ignore. Then Everly's lips parted, ever so slightly, and Henry got the feeling that she was going to tell him something.

Say it, he thought. *Whatever it is, just tell me. I'm still me. We're still* us. *Just closer...*better...*than we were before.*

Then Everly's eyes flitted over Henry's shoulder, where his bags were piled by the door. After *Veil* had them delivered, he'd left them there while he'd finished cooking dinner. Everly stared at the luggage for a beat, and when she looked at him again, her expression closed like a book.

Henry's own words from just a moment ago came back to him.

Not everyone leaves, E.

He'd left, though. He'd put her in a cab and he'd gone straight to the airport, just like always.

It wasn't like that, though. It was what she'd wanted...

Friends forever.

Was it, though? Was it what either of them had really wanted?

Henry had no idea. All he knew was that right here, right now, sitting beside Everly, he felt more at home than he had in months...years. And for once in his life, he was in no hurry whatsoever to pack up and go.

Chapter Seven

Everly woke up the following morning to find Henry lounging against the kitchen counter in nothing but a pair of navy pajama bottoms, sipping coffee as if he owned the place.

"Hey," he said with a wink. "Feeling better this morning?"

"Morning. I feel great, actually," Everly said, struggling not to stare at his abs. Was it possible they'd gotten even more defined while he'd been in Bora-Bora? What had he been doing down there? Cracking coconuts with his core muscles?

She opened her mouth to tell him to put some clothes on. Friends didn't walk around half naked in front of each other. Not once had she seen Chandler do this in Monica's kitchen. Not even Joey, which was really saying something.

But before she could manage to string together a coherent sentence, Henry pushed off the counter and reached for something behind her. His sudden closeness made her head spin in a distinctly *non*friendly way. He smelled like rich espresso and fresh, clean soap. Everly had to stop herself from taking in a long, leisurely inhale.

"I made you a little something for breakfast," Henry said, presenting her with a plate topped with a toasted bagel sliced neatly in half and slathered with a generous amount of cream cheese and thinly sliced strawberries. "I toasted it until it was barely crunchy on top, just the way you like it."

"Henry," Everly said, glaring down at the plate. He really needed to stop doing things like this. It was getting…confusing.

He'd been living in her apartment less than twenty-four hours, and already she was beginning to enjoy being taken care of. Which was bad. *Very* bad. It would only make things that much harder six weeks from now when he jetted off someplace exotic and Everly was stuck at home toasting her own bagels and eating pasta from a cardboard box.

Henry's gaze narrowed. "I think the words you're looking for are *thank* and *you*."

"Sorry. Thank you." Everly took the plate, bit into the bagel and immediately knew it wasn't one of the frozen ones that had been collecting frost at the back of her freezer for the past six months. This was one of the *good* bagels from the place down the street that she loved so much. Damn him. "But you've got to stop feeding me like this. You're going to spoil me."

He arched a brow. "Would that really be so terrible?"

Yes. One thousand percent yes. "I'm just saying, it's not necessary. Anyway, you know I usually skip breakfast."

"Says the woman who fainted in the middle of a staff meeting yesterday." Henry shot her a mighty eye roll.

"So this is a work thing, then?" Everly took another bite. "The fancy guest editor doesn't want one of the junior reporters fainting on the job and disrupting the office?"

"Something like that," Henry said and sipped his coffee without breaking her gaze.

Everly willed herself not to swoon. She blamed the bagels. And her apparently raging pregnancy hormones. In any event, she needed to get out of there before the waistband on his pajama pants shifted any lower.

"Thanks for the bagel." She shoved what was left of it into her mouth and placed her plate in the sink. "But I've got to go ahead and get going. I have an early meeting with Addison this morning."

"See you at the office later," he said and made a *cheers* motion with his coffee cup.

"See you," Everly said and cast a parting glance

at his bare chest before spinning on the heel of her stiletto and walking away. *Don't say it. Do* not. "Oh, and Henry?"

"Yes?"

"Would you mind investing in a pajama top?" Dang, she'd said it. She cleared her throat, hitched her handbag higher onto her shoulder and feigned indifference to his abs, still annoyingly on full display. "Unless you want your old college sweatshirt back. I'm sure I've got it around here somewhere."

Everly knew exactly where to find that sweatshirt. It was as soft as a teddy bear and folded neatly at the very top of her middle dresser drawer, right beside her favorite cashmere joggers. No way she was giving it up. He'd given it to her fair and square when he'd moved to London, and if he wanted it back, he'd have to pry it out of her cold, dead hands.

The corner of Henry's lips hitched into an amused grin. He didn't say anything—he didn't have to.

That smirk of his said it all.

Fashion closet. 15 minutes.

Everly had banged out the group text message to Daphne and Addison the moment the apartment door clicked shut behind her. There'd been no need to specify that it was an emergency. The gravity of the situation was more than clear.

The *Veil* fashion closet was legendary—not just because it housed rack upon rack of the finest de-

signer wedding gowns in the world but also because
it was Everly, Daphne and Addison's meeting place
of choice when one of them was experiencing a crisis.

"Closet" was an understatement, really. The *Veil*
closet was about the size of a Manhattan one-bedroom apartment—a *large* one-bedroom. The walls
were lined top to bottom with custom shelves that
housed row upon row of designer shoes, while the
rest of the space was a neatly organized maze of rolling racks stuffed to overflowing with bridal gowns
and bridesmaid's dresses. Somewhere in all of that
puffy organza was a small rack of men's bespoke
tuxedos...allegedly. No one had actually set eyes on
it before. Its existence was either a *Veil* urban leg-
end, or the tuxes had simply been swallowed up by
mountains of tulle and sequins.

The purpose of the closet was to store articles
of clothing that had been gifted to the magazine or
were simply on loan, either for photoshoots or in-
person functions hosted by *Veil*. But with its over-
stuffed round ottoman covered in white satin damask
and situated smack in the middle of the room, it
was also the perfect place to have a meltdown in the
workplace. Something about being surrounded by
all of those gorgeous dresses just made everything
feel a little better. Or maybe it was because wedding gowns symbolized hope and new beginnings.
Everly couldn't remember exactly how or why the

tradition started, but whenever one of the members of their little *Veil* crew needed to vent or cry or just sit in companionable silence, they met in the closet.

So naturally, Addison and Daphne had received her text with the proper amount of reverence and were already waiting for Everly on the tufted ottoman when she arrived at the office.

"Spill." Addison patted the spot beside her. "What's wrong?"

Daphne handed Everly a steaming paper cup wrapped in a familiar pink cardboard sleeve as she collapsed onto the ottoman with a sigh.

"Thank you." Everly took a giant gulp from the cup. Ahh, a decaf cupcake latte. Just what she needed...especially since she hadn't lingered in the kitchen long enough to make herself a cup of coffee, what with the coffee maker being blocked by a certain half-naked male. "To answer your question, *everything* is wrong."

Daphne bit her lip. "It's not the baby, is it?"

"Oh, no. The baby is fine, thank goodness. I actually feel pretty good this morning. I got a lot of sleep yesterday and plenty to eat." Everly pressed a hand to her stomach. She was dressed in her favorite high-waisted black trousers and a crisp white wraparound blouse that tied in a big bow at her left hip. She wondered how long she had until people started noticing the little bump she'd studied in front of the bathroom mirror this morning. Not just *people*, but one person specifically. "It's Henry. He's driving me nuts."

"You're kidding." Addison snorted into her coffee cup, which Everly knew without even asking was fully caffeinated. Addison was a rich, dark espresso sort of girl. No fancy flavors, no nonsense. A mini Colette in the making. "You two always get along. You're like two peas in a pod. It's actually pretty annoying sometimes."

"Yeah, it is." Daphne nodded and twirled a lock of pink hair around one of her fingers. Her French manicure was decorated with pearls placed in the center of each fingernail. "*Trés* annoying."

Everly felt herself frown. "Why is it annoying? You two have other friends that I don't mind hanging out with from time to time."

"Not like Henry. He just seems to get you, even more than we do. It's like he can see straight inside your head," Addison said.

Daphne nodded. "You have so many inside jokes that sometimes it feels like you're speaking your own secret language."

"It's actually sort of sweet." Addison gave Everly a shoulder bump. "Annoying when I have no clue what you two are going on about—or when you refuse to answer my calls after being left at the altar, even though I know for a fact that you allowed Henry to check on you—but sweet, nonetheless."

Everly choked a little on her latte. "You know I was with Henry after the wedding?"

"When you wouldn't answer your phone, Daphne

and I were worried. So was Mom. So I texted Henry to see if he knew where you were." Addison's shoulders lifted, then fell. "He texted me back a while later and said not to worry. He had things covered."

He certainly had.

Everly bit her lip. Henry hadn't been the one who'd initiated intimacy. That was all on her.

"How could he possibly be driving you nuts?" Daphne asked, dragging Everly's attention back to the present.

"He made me pasta last night. *Homemade* pasta—as in, he kneaded the dough and everything." Everly's stomach growled just thinking about it. That had been the best meal of her entire life.

Addison and Daphne exchanged a glance.

"And?" Daphne prompted.

Everly sighed. "Then he put on *Breakfast at Tiffany's.*"

"Again?" Addison groaned. "Why? You've seen it at least a hundred times by now."

That was precisely the point. It was Everly's comfort watch—a fact that Henry not only knew but also respected. He didn't even make fun of her when she got teary-eyed while Audrey Hepburn sang "Moon River." Every. Single. Time.

Daphne held up a hand. "Wait, I'm confused. Pasta from scratch? Your favorite movie? Am I missing something? Because those things don't sound annoying at all. They seem really nice."

"This morning he even made me breakfast," Everly spat.

Addison arched a brow. "Clearly he's a monster. How will you ever stand living with him for six whole weeks?"

"Did I mention he was *shirtless*?" Everly slung back the rest of her coffee.

Daphne bit back a smile. "Wait a minute. What's going on here?"

Addison's forehead scrunched. "Surely you've seen Henry shirtless before."

"Unless…" Daphne's mouth dropped open, then she let out an earsplitting squeal. "Noooooo. It can't be. He's not…he's *Henry*."

Everly let out a shuddering exhale. Daphne had clearly figured out where the conversation was headed. She sort of wished Addison had, too, so she wouldn't have to say it out loud. Everly still hadn't quite processed it herself, and telling people would make it real.

Like the sweet little bump you're hiding under that big white bow isn't *real?*

"What?" Addison shook her head. "What am I missing?"

Everly took a deep breath and shifted her gaze from a clearly ecstatic Daphne back to her sister. "Henry's the baby's father."

Addison went still—as unmoving as a statue—as she processed Everly's words. Everly waited a beat and then waved a hand in front of her sister's face. When at last Addison blinked, her eyes widened an alarming amount. "But...but...he's *Henry.*"

Why did everyone keep saying that? Everly was well aware of the man's name.

"You two are best friends, not lovers," Addison said bluntly.

Now that the shock was beginning to wear off, they were beginning to get down to the crux of the problem.

"Exactly." Everly stood and began pacing circles around the ottoman. She couldn't sit still anymore. Nervous energy was spilling from her every pore. She wondered if her latte had truly been decaf.

"I...wow." A hysterical burst of laughter escaped Addison. "Sorry, this is just a lot to process."

"What Addison said. We just assumed Gregory was the father." Daphne looked Everly up and down. She couldn't seem to wipe the silly grin off her face. "Never in my life would I have guessed that you slept with anyone other than him. I mean, look at you."

Everly's footsteps paused. "What's that supposed to mean?"

Daphne shrugged. "Nothing derogatory at all, hon. You're just not exactly a one-night-stand kind of girl."

"Exactly. You're definitely the white picket fences type," Addison said. "And you were about to marry the guy."

That's right. She certainly was.

Thank God for small favors.

Actually, it had been a giant favor. Huge. Unspeakably enormous. Everly couldn't even imagine being married to Gregory right now.

"Well, I didn't," Everly said quietly.

For the first time in years, she didn't know what her life would look like from one day to the next. Losing her dad had turned everything so upside down that Everly longed for security. She *needed* it. So long as she knew what to expect, the rug could never be so cruelly ripped out from under her again.

She liked things neat and orderly. She was the columnist who people came to when they were confused and they needed advice. She wasn't supposed to *be* the one whose life was in tatters.

"So...you and Henry?" Daphne tilted her head. "I can see it. In fact, this has probably been a long time coming. Are you guys a couple now?"

Everly stumbled on an invisible spot on the closet floor. Probably a stray seed pearl or something. "What? No. Absolutely not. He doesn't even know about the baby."

"He has no idea?" Addison gaped at her. "At all?"

"None whatsoever."

Daphne's right eyebrow quirked closer to her pink highlighted hairline. "Then why is he here, living in your apartment, making shirtless coffee and working at your magazine?"

"Honestly?" Everly sighed. "I have no idea."

He'd said he'd taken the temporary job at *Veil* because he thought it would be fun working together. But that didn't explain the lack of pajama top, and it certainly didn't explain the lingering sparks that kept flickering between them. Or the way she'd caught him looking at her during the movie last night when Audrey Hepburn and George Peppard kissed in the rain…like he'd wanted to break down her walls and show her what it meant to be loved by someone who really understood her, someone who loved her with his whole heart.

Someone who'd stay.

She swallowed hard. Henry wasn't that person. He never had been, never would be. She was letting her favorite movie and a few pregnancy hormones go to her head…or her heart. Possibly both.

"Everly, you have to tell him," Addison said.

Everly nodded. *I know.* She tried to say it, but she couldn't get the words out around the lump that had just formed in her throat.

Daphne reached out to squeeze her hand. "Hon, it's going to be okay. Henry is amazing. He's been so sweet, taking such good care of you, all because you fainted. Just imagine how great he'll be once he finds out about the baby."

That was precisely the problem, though. Everly didn't want Henry falling all over himself to take care of her. It would only make it that much harder when he left or, heaven forbid, when she started having feelings for him that went beyond friendship.

Not everyone leaves, E.

He'd looked so serious when he'd said those words. So earnest. She'd come so close to telling him about the baby right then and there.

Then she'd spotted his luggage out of the corner of her eye, and she'd remembered who Henry was. Not just her best friend but the man who'd made his dying father a promise to see the world. He'd spent his entire adult life honoring that promise, and Everly couldn't be the person who took that away from him. She wouldn't.

"You two will figure this out," Addison said.

Everly glanced up to meet her sister's gaze, but her attention snagged on a pale pink ribbon behind Addison's head. She let her eyes follow the trail of blush pink all the way to the waist of a beautifully crafted wedding gown. *Her* wedding gown.

Everly hadn't set eyes on the Marchesa dress since the morning after sleeping with Henry, when she'd done her bridal walk of shame through the lobby of the Plaza. After she'd gotten home, Addison had come over, and upon Everly's request, she'd swept the designer gown out of Everly's sight and returned it to *Veil*. And now here it was, a breathtaking reminder of the fateful night everything had changed.

When she looked at the dress now, it didn't remind her of Gregory or the wedding or the sting of humiliation she'd experienced in that gilded, glittering ballroom. All she could see as her gaze swept over the soft pink ribbon was Henry giving the sash a gentle tug…his hands unlacing the bodice…his reverent expression as the gown had slipped from her body and fallen to the floor in a whisper of anticipation. So much about that night was a blur, but Everly would never forget how it felt when Henry saw her standing before him bared and breathless.

Never in her life had anyone looked at Everly like that before—like she was the most beautiful woman in the world. Treasured. Desired.

Loved.

Everly averted her gaze from the Marchesa gown and reminded herself that she'd been wrong about a lot of things lately. She couldn't be trusted to advise *anyone*, least of all herself.

"Just tell him," Addison said. "You have nothing at all to worry about."

If only it were the truth.

Chapter Eight

Immediately following the crisis meeting in the fashion closet, Everly found herself engaged in a discussion that could only be described as mortifying—not with Henry but with her boss.

"I don't understand." The polite, professional smile that Everly had glued onto her face as she'd entered Colette's office dimmed...by a lot. "You want me to write about a dog wedding?"

Surely she'd just heard Colette wrong. This was *Veil*, not *Dog Fancy*. While Everly wasn't allowed to work on her column, she was supposed to be writing about bespoke bridal fashion, decadent cakes or—worst-case scenario—something dull, like the most elegant font choices for save-the-date cards.

In short, she was supposed to be writing about *weddings*, not Weimaraners.

"Yes. It will be a precious addition to the June issue, don't you think?" Colette smiled. Everly was pretty sure her boss wasn't actively trying to look condescending, but come on. Never in her entire tenure at *Veil* had Everly seen Colette look so thrilled to be discussing canine couture.

"Precious," Everly echoed. "Yes, for certain. But, um, I was hoping for something a little more…" *Sane.* That was the word she was looking for. She didn't dare say it, though. "…fashion-forward."

Colette arched a single perfectly groomed eyebrow. "The bride is a purebred Cavalier King Charles spaniel, and she's being dressed by Vera Wang."

Everly blinked. Okay, then.

"The wedding is a fundraiser for Manhattan Pet Rescue, and it takes place this evening in Central Park. We're sending a photographer, and you'll write the accompanying copy. Two hundred fifty words, and I'll need it by tomorrow morning. Any questions?" Colette said.

Two hundred fifty words. That was it? She wasn't writing an article. She was writing a glorified caption for a pet pictorial.

Everly held up a finger. "I do have one quick question. This is a wonderful opportunity, obviously." She didn't want to seem ungrateful, but this couldn't be her only contribution to the June edition. It just couldn't. "I'd love to take on something else for the June issue. I've prepared a few pitches that I'd be happy to present—"

Colette held up a hand. "Everly, please. Let's just see how you do on this assignment and proceed from there, shall we?"

Everly swallowed. In one fell swoop, she'd gone from being a relationship guru to covering dog weddings. How the mighty had fallen.

"Now that everything is settled, I'm going to need you to get back to your desk. I've got my interview with our guest editor in just a few minutes." Colette opened a file folder, revealing a copy of *Wanderlust* magazine with Henry's picture splashed across the cover. The photo had captured him zip-lining through the Amazon Rainforest, glistening with sweat and grinning from ear to ear. A baby sloth was tucked against his chest in a sling, because of course it was.

Everly stared at the tiny animal. Maybe if she stared at it hard enough, she could imagine it morphing into a human infant. Alas, no.

She was being ridiculous. Henry was a wonderful, loving man. He'd never once, in all the times she'd known him, said a negative word about babies or small children.

Nor had he ever uttered a word about settling down and having a family.

"Everly?" Colette drummed her fingernails on

her desk, once again eyeing Everly with a combination of pity and annoyance. Everly couldn't help but notice that the scales were beginning to tip in favor of annoyance.

She scrambled to her feet, smiling hard. Smiling like she'd been waiting her entire life to witness a pair of companion animals exchange sacred vows.

"Back to my desk. I'm going. And don't worry—the dog piece will be brilliant. Hopeful…optimistic…*romantic*," Everly gushed. Were those words seriously coming out of her mouth? "I promise."

If tackling this humiliating assignment was the way to get her career back on track, then fine. She'd do it. She'd walk across hot coals if she had to.

Everly turned to go. Just as she was making her way through the entrance to Colette's office, Henry entered. He met her in the doorframe, pausing to grin down at her.

"Hi, there," he said, eyes twinkling.

Every last bit of Everly's breath bottled in her throat. He was so close that she could smell his aftershave and the lingering aroma of freshly ground coffee beans clinging to his finely tailored suit. The coffee that he'd consumed from *her* coffee maker in *her* kitchen. Shirtless.

Breathe, she told herself. All she could seem to think about was the answer he'd given her when she'd asked him why he wanted to take the temporary job at *Veil*.

Because of you, obviously.

A delicious little shiver snaked its way up her spine. "Hi, there," she said back.

"You left in an awfully big hurry this morning." Henry's voice was velvety soft. It made Everly want to curl up in his lap and rest her head against his firm chest. "If I didn't know better, I might think you were trying to avoid me."

Everly laughed a little too loud. She was vaguely aware of Colette's head turning in their direction in her periphery. "Don't be silly. Of course I'm not trying to avoid you. You were just running late, as per usual."

"Even later, what with having to stop and buy a pajama shirt on the way to work," he said in a barely audible murmur, and the words zinged through her like a shooting star. Dazzling and white-hot.

Everly tingled, from head to toe.

Had they always flirted like this? Everly honestly didn't know. If so, it had been innocent, playful banter. Hadn't it?

It had certainly never affected her quite like this before. She couldn't remember the last time she'd felt this...*unsettled*...in another man's presence. Like she was made of stardust, shining from the inside out.

That would be never, *and you know it.*

She squared her shoulders and somehow managed to drag her attention away from the quiet intensity of Henry's gaze. Her eyes darted to the knot in his tie, which was no help whatsoever. Everly had always been a sucker for a perfectly tied half Windsor.

How does he manage to look as perfectly at ease in a coat and tie as he does zip-lining through the rainforest with a wild animal strapped to his chest? It was a disturbingly attractive quality—which, for reasons beyond her comprehension, Everly had failed to fully appreciate until six weeks ago.

"Don't you have an interview to get to?" she said, lifting her gaze back to his eyes. *It's only Henry*, she reminded herself, but her racing pulse didn't seem to get the message.

"Don't you have a fashion show or someplace else to be?" he countered.

"As a matter of fact, I do." *I do…*wedding words. Words that, for the life of her, Everly could no longer imagine uttering to Gregory Hoyt. "I'm off to a dog wedding. The bride is wearing Vera Wang."

Henry's gaze narrowed. "I suddenly have a lot of questions."

So do I, and they've got nothing to do with dog nuptials.

Everly gave him a fluttery wave, meant to be mysterious as she slipped past him, toward her cubicle.

Ha! She could feel his eyes on her as she sashayed back to her desk in her favorite stilettos—the ones with the mesh polka-dot detailing and ultrapointed toes. At last she'd turned the tables, and now Henry was the one thrown off-balance. *He* was the one left wondering what was going on in *her* head. He was the one left feeling achingly unsatisfied after a simple interaction between friends, not her.

At least that's what Everly tried to tell herself, even as the urge to look over her shoulder one last time at him told her otherwise.

Having never attended a dog wedding before, Everly wasn't sure what to expect. But no amount of speculation would have prepared her for the sight that greeted her later that afternoon in Central Park's Conservatory Garden.

For starters, as the only formal garden in the entire park, the Conservatory Garden was prime wedding real estate. Actual human beings waited months, if not years, to exchange vows there. Central Park was always gorgeous in the spring, when the cherry blossoms were in full bloom. Delicate pink and white petals swirled through the air like snowflakes as Everly made her way down Terrace Drive where it bordered Pilgrim Hill. But when she reached the North Garden in the Conservatory, the sight before her was more magical than ever.

With its intricately shaped topiaries and curved hedges, the garden itself looked like it was straight out of Versailles. Everly had always particularly loved the bronze Three Dancing Maidens fountain that stood in the center of the North Garden's lily pond, so whimsically ethereal. Today, though, the garden was decked out like she'd never seen it before. Carpets of blush and red tulips surrounded the pond, and the leafy archway that was usually covered in ivy and vines was now an explosion of colorful blossoms. The air was thick with the scent of hyacinth and pink peonies.

And the dogs! They were everywhere, of every variety—from tiny Chihuahuas in bow ties to a pair of striking black-and-white Harlequin Great Danes with wreaths of white flowers around their thick necks. Everly actually found herself smiling. Maybe covering this story wouldn't be so bad, after all. As garden weddings went, this was one of the most stunning ones she'd ever seen.

First up, she needed to locate the bride and groom, two dogs currently up for adoption at Manhattan Pet Rescue. The *Veil* photographer had arrived separately, over an hour ago and texted Everly with the supersecret identity of the wedding party. As Colette mentioned, the bride was a young Cavalier King Charles spaniel with a chestnut-and-white coat—known as Blenheim in fancy dog circles—and she was apparently marrying a shaggy schnauzer mix with an impressive silver mustache. Everly was already getting strong *Lady and the Tramp* vibes from the pairing. The photos were sure to be adorable.

"Excuse me?" Everly stopped a woman wearing a Manhattan Pet Rescue T-shirt and pressed khaki trousers as she dashed past her on the cobblestone walkway. "I'm here from *Veil Magazine*. We're doing a story on the wedding. Could you tell me where I can find whoever is in charge?"

The woman sighed, looking a bit frazzled. Perhaps Lady was being a bridezilla. "That would be the wedding planner and the chairperson of the fundraising committee." She tipped her head toward a white tent set up around the corner from the floral arch. "They're in there. But brace yourself. At the moment, things are a little…tense. I'm trying to find the shelter's trainer so he can intervene."

"Thank you so much," Everly said. When it came to wedding stress, she'd seen and heard it all. Her column had been a treasure trove of drama. It was almost funny to think that even dogs weren't immune.

She was decidedly less amused, however, when she stepped inside the tent.

The little Cavalier King Charles spaniel—resplendent in her tiny Vera Wang—shook like a leaf, cowering in the corner. A pitiful whine escaped the precious dog as she peered up at Everly with the saddest puppy dog eyes she'd ever seen. Everly glanced up in search of someone who could help, but the half dozen people in the tent were engaged in a heated conversation. None of them appeared to be paying a lick of attention to the pup.

"Excuse me." Everly cleared her throat. "Why is the bride crying?"

The voices around her stuttered to a halt. A shaggy

gray dog—the groom, presumably—let out a squeaky dog yawn on the other side of the tent. Then the groom dropped into a down position with his head resting on his paws and sighed, long and loud.

A tall man dressed in a tuxedo jacket and a Manhattan Pet Rescue T-shirt looked Everly up and down. "I beg your pardon?"

"Whining," Everly clarified. "I meant why is the bride whining? The poor thing seems terrified."

Everly knew next to nothing about dogs. But she knew suffering when she saw it, and she certainly knew a fair bit about wedding-night cold feet. She had no idea what specifically was wrong, but she had the sudden urge to gather the fluffy dog into her arms and whisk her away to the Plaza's honeymoon suite with a can of squirt cheese and a box of Ritz Crackers.

The man's gaze narrowed. "And you are?"

The little Cavalier pressed her trembling form against Everly's legs. With every sad little shudder, Everly felt herself getting more and more enraged on her behalf. *You need a man of honor, you poor thing.* Her gaze locked with the Cavalier's soft brown eyes. *You need a Henry.*

She bent to scoop the dog into her arms. "My name is Everly England."

"We're going to need you to put the dog back down. That gown is couture," one of the women flanking tuxedo guy said.

"I know a designer wedding gown when I see one, and sorry, no. I'm not letting the bride go. Can't anyone see that she's upset?" Everly could hear her voice going shrill, but she couldn't seem to stop it. Somewhere in the back of her head, she was vaguely aware that she was on the verge of digging an even deeper hole for herself at *Veil*, but that didn't seem important. Not at this precise moment, when a dog was being forced to marry a schnauzer, seemingly against her will.

What is wrong with you? This is a softball writing assignment. Colette is going to fire you if you mess it up. They're dogs.

"She's upset because the groom snapped at her, but it's going to be fine. This event is our biggest fundraiser of the year. We just need to get these two down the aisle without further incident." Tuxedo guy glanced from the bride to the groom and back again. "It would be helpful if you released the dog. Miss England, is it?"

He could *not* be serious.

"The groom tried to *bite* her?" Everly held the dog closer to her chest. The Cavalier's heart fluttered like a baby bird trapped in a cage. "And you're trying to make her marry him anyway?"

No way. Not going to happen. Not while Everly was here.

"This is an event designed to raise money for charity. After today, she never has to see him again."

The man pinched the bridge of his nose, as if Everly's mere presence was more than he could possibly tolerate, even among moody canines dressed in clothes that most human beings couldn't afford. "You do realize this isn't a real marriage? They're dogs."

"Does that matter? Clearly he doesn't want to marry her." Everly waved a hand at the schnauzer, whom she'd dubbed 'Gregory' in her imagination. "The wedding is off."

"With all due respect, you can't cancel the wedding. We don't even know who you are or why you're here," one of the women in attendance said.

"I think we might need to call security," someone else added.

"Go ahead," Everly said, glaring at the groom, who had the audacity to roll over onto his back and begin snoring. He was probably dreaming about his doggy yacht club. Everly was certain of it. "But she's not marrying him. You can't make her."

Everly was no longer sure who was trembling harder now—the Cavalier or her. She must have been experiencing some sort of post-traumatic wedding episode. The only way through it seemed to be saving the poor doggy bride from having to go through with marrying a dog who'd clearly just rejected her.

"It's not you," she whispered to the dog. "It's him. You're perfect."

The Cavalier made a sweet snuffling sound, and

when Everly glanced down at her, the pup's little pink tongue swiped the side of Everly's cheek.

"It's going to be okay," Everly murmured.

"Wait a minute. Did you say your name was Everly England?" One of the volunteers crossed her arms and peered at Everly as if she were a science experiment. "As in, Everly England the advice columnist from *Veil* who got left at the altar at that fancy wedding at the Plaza?"

The bottom dropped out of Everly's stomach. She shouldn't have made that comment about designer gowns. It had likely been a dead giveaway. Then again, perhaps she shouldn't be making a spectacle of herself by busting up a dog wedding.

Colette was right, wasn't she? Everly no longer believed in love. That's why she'd been running around for weeks acting like the universe had yelled loudly directly into her ear, "Should anyone here present know of any reason that this couple should not be joined in holy matrimony, speak now or forever hold your peace."

Except the universe had never said that. No one had, but Everly couldn't seem to keep a lid on her peace no matter how hard she tried.

Perhaps she'd *never* believed in love, and she'd just been going through the motions with Gregory. He'd figured out how profoundly broken she was, and he'd cut and run just in the nick of time.

It was a sobering possibility, to say the least. Everly's throat went dry as a bone just thinking about it. She felt like she'd swallowed a mouthful of sand from one of the gorgeous beaches Henry frequented.

"You *are* her," the woman said, eyes going wide. "I've seen your picture in the magazine."

This day can't possibly get any worse, Everly thought just as two uniformed security officers swept into the tent. Wrong again, apparently.

The security guards both immediately zeroed in on Everly, as if they fully expected her to try and abscond with both the Cavalier King Charles spaniel and her designer doggy gown. She very well might have, if not for the polka-dot stilettos.

"Did someone here call about a disturbance?" the taller security guard asked, hand resting on the Taser attached to his utility belt.

Everly pressed her lips to the Cavalier's silky ear. "It's going to be okay," she said again.

Only this time, she wasn't sure if she was talking to the dog or to herself.

Chapter Nine

Henry's interview lasted the better part of the afternoon. When Colette first mentioned that she wanted to include a profile of him in the honeymoon pullout section of the June issue, he'd hoped she might give the assignment to Everly.

No such luck. Colette wanted to write the piece herself, and even if she hadn't, Everly had apparently been banished to some weird form of wedding reporter exile, where she was expected to write about absurd things like dog weddings.

He still wasn't altogether sure she hadn't been pulling his leg. Henry fully believed the reason Everly's cubicle sat empty when he emerged from Colette's office was because Everly was sitting in the front row of a bridal fashion show somewhere. He could picture her perched on the edge of her seat, back as straight and supple as a ballerina's and feet crossed primly at the ankles. Everly had always carried herself with a natural grace that made her appear as though she'd been to charm school. Men typically loved it. It drove them mad, which in turn, drove Henry mad. Even after he'd taken up permanent residence in the friend zone, he'd always felt overly protective of Everly when she captured a man's attention.

Or maybe you were just jealous all along, you fool.

Henry tugged at the knot in his tie. He needed to stop thinking about Everly's empty cubicle and get to work. Being tied up in the interview all day meant his inbox was overflowing with emails, and he still needed to choose the top ten honeymoon locations he wanted to feature in the issue. The last time he'd taken a crack at the list, he'd been unable to narrow it down below nineteen breathtaking vacation spots. Once he selected the locations, he'd need to pull photos from his various trips for *Wanderlust* and do a write-up for each. And all of that was on top of editing the issue's other honeymoon-related content.

Henry didn't need to be mooning over his best friend. He needed quality time at his desk, and he needed caffeine. Lots of it.

He strode through the *Veil* lobby en route to the break room, home to a European espresso machine most often frequented by Henry and Addison. But as he passed the reception desk, he overheard a snippet of conversation that gave him pause.

"Let me make sure I'm understanding you correctly." Ivy, the receptionist, grimaced into her phone. "One of our reporters is being accused of...dognapping?"

Henry's footsteps slowed. He felt himself frown as he turned back toward Ivy's desk.

"Yes, that does sound like a problem," Ivy said, nodding at whatever the person on the other end of the line was saying. "Apologies on behalf of *Veil.* Perhaps our editor in chief—"

Henry cleared his throat. "Ivy, let's not bother Colette with this."

The receptionist glanced up at him, relief etched in her features. "Hold just one second, please," she said into the phone.

Henry flashed her a wink and held out his hand. "Give it to me. I can handle whatever this is."

"You're sure?" Ivy asked.

Oh, he was definitely sure.

After a brief conversation, Henry took the *Veil* car service and made it to the Conservatory Garden in Central Park in record time, where an attempted dognapping was indeed in progress. As he suspected, Everly appeared to be the perpetrator.

"Henry?" Her eyes were huge in her face, starbright and brimming with tears as she looked at him from across the white tent as he stalked inside. She clutched the dog in her arms as tightly as a child with a favorite teddy bear. "W-what are you doing here?"

He took a brief survey of the situation. Two weary security officers flanked Everly on either side, while a small group of people dressed in a peculiar combination of Manhattan Pet Rescue T-shirts mixed with formal wear looked all too eager for her to be carted off to jail. A scruffy schnauzer mix trotted over to Henry and pawed at his shoe. It would have been cute if not for the fact that the entire scene felt like a Disney movie gone horribly, horribly wrong.

Henry offered everyone assembled a solicitous smile as he crossed to the other side of the tent to Everly's side.

"Not to worry, darling. I'm here to help," he said under his breath. "Just smile and try not to look so much like a well-dressed Cruella De Vil."

A hint of a smile danced on Everly's bow-shaped lips.

"Cruella is actually a fashion icon—the ill-advised puppy coat being a notable exception," she whispered. "Obviously."

That's my girl, Henry thought. She wasn't about to pass up an opportunity for fashion commentary, even when on the brink of tears.

"Obviously," he echoed. Then he blew Everly a nearly invisible kiss.

The dog in her arms let out a sigh as Henry prepared himself to do whatever it took to get Everly out of this mess.

Why did he get the feeling that he was about to adopt a Cavalier King Charles spaniel in a wedding dress?

"Thank you, again," Everly said an hour later as they sat on opposite ends of Everly's curved velvet sofa, watching the dog sniff every square inch of their apartment.

Her apartment, Henry reminded himself. This entire arrangement was only temporary, and the expiration date felt like it was barreling toward him at warp speed. The newly adopted Cavalier King Charles already had a more permanent place in Everly's everyday life than he did.

"I'm sure you would've handled things on your own, eventually," Henry said, and he firmly believed it. Beneath the glamorous exterior, Everly could be tough as nails—as evidenced by the fact that a schnauzer mix had just married a last-minute poodle stand-in in Central Park.

She was just going through a rough patch. It happened to everyone, but when it happened to Everly, Henry couldn't see straight. He had the urge to fix things even though he knew that was probably an evolutionary holdover from caveman days, and women didn't men to swoop in and solve their problems. Or maybe the need he had to fix things for

Everly was something else entirely…something that felt an awful lot like love.

Friendship! the rational side of his brain screamed. Henry's teeth clenched. Sometimes he really wanted to tell his rational side to take a hike.

"I can't believe the wedding planner called *Veil*." Everly bit her lip. "I'm going to get called into Colette's office again tomorrow. And this time, I think she's really going to fire me."

"You're not getting fired." Henry shook his head. Averted his gaze.

Ivy had been all too happy to assure him that she wouldn't mention the phone call to Colette. No one in the office enjoyed delivering bad news to the mercurial editor in chief.

Henry had managed to secure the silence and cooperation of the Manhattan Pet Rescue board members by including a sizable donation to their organization, over and above the astronomical pet placement fee they'd quoted him for adopting the Cavalier King Charles spaniel. The amount of money he'd Venmoed the pet charity had been truly eye-watering but worth every penny when he'd told Everly she could take the dog home with her. The only caveat had been the swift return of the Vera Wang doggy gown, which Everly had been all too happy to give up.

"I don't know what got into me. I just couldn't let her marry that schnauzer." Everly groaned and dropped her head into her hands. "Listen to me! I've lost my mind. I put my entire career and reputation in jeopardy over a pretend dog wedding."

"I don't know. That minister seemed pretty legit," Henry said, scooting closer to give her knee a gentle nudge with his. "Something tells me Tramp and his poodle are in it for the long haul."

"You're ridiculous," Everly said, but her eyes sparkled at him in a way that reminded him of fizzy pink champagne and crisp white hotel sheets.

"You love it, and you know it," he said, fully expecting an eye roll or a playful swat in return.

Instead, Everly reached for his hand, wove her fingers through his and offered him a smile that was so tender, so gentle that his heart turned over in his chest. "I mean it, Henry. Thank you for being there today."

"Always," he said.

Friends forever.

The words hung heavy in the air, like a thundercloud—unspoken yet swollen with memories and meaning and so many feelings they both kept doing their best to deny.

Henry ran the pad of his thumb over the soft, sensitive center of Everly's palm and watched as her eyes changed from glittering violet to a thunderous purple. She was looking at him with bedroom eyes—eyes that made him want to do distinctly *un*friendly things to her.

He swallowed hard.

How long were they going to play this game? How many more days of working together and nights of sleeping in the same apartment were they going to keep pretending that what happened between them hadn't meant something when, in fact, it had meant *everything*?

"E," he said, hoping…praying…for a moment of raw, unguarded honesty. She was his friend, but she was also so much more. They'd never had trouble talking to each other before.

But that was then, and this was now.

"What do you think I should name her?" Everly said, dragging her gaze away from his and focusing on the dog.

The Cavalier lit up like a Christmas tree every time Everly looked at her. Her tail wagged as she trotted toward Everly with her tongue lolling happily out of the side of her mouth.

Henry didn't need to give the question more than a moment's thought. "Holly Golightly."

For a minute there, when he'd walked into the tent in Central Park and found her clinging to that dog, Henry had the uncanny feeling he'd stumbled into Everly's favorite movie. In *Breakfast at Tiffany's*, Holly insisted that she and her pet cat were the same—both fiercely independent, both unattached to anyone or anything.

Everly and the Cavalier were like Holly and Cat.

It didn't take a genius to know why Everly identified with the dog. She'd seen herself in those melting brown eyes and trembling little body—frightened, alone and lost. Wanting so desperately to belong to someone but at the same time too scared to give in and let go.

There was no doubt in Henry's mind that Everly would've gone through with her wedding vows to Gregory if he hadn't bolted. But in the hours after the wedding…in those dark, delicious moments when she'd given herself to Henry—body, mind and soul—he'd come to realize the truth about her and Gregory: she didn't really love him. She loved the idea of a safe, secure life, but she'd never, ever been head over heels for Gregory Hoyt. She'd never even let him see her the way that Henry did. Her vulnerability was something she only ever showed to him and him alone. It had been that way for as long as they'd known each other. All the years. All the tears. All the late-night phone calls from opposite sides of the world…

Now they were here, together again. Just like old times.

Except for the part where he couldn't stop wanting her.

"Holly Golightly. I love it." Everly beamed as she bent to gather the dog into her arms. "How about it, Holly? Is that what we should call you?"

The Cavalier let out a yip and nuzzled her round

little head against Everly's cheek, prompting Everly to close her eyes and rest her face against Holly's.

Henry's chest suddenly felt so tight that he could barely breathe.

"What?" Everly said, as her eyelashes fluttered open.

"I've never seen you like this before. I rather like it." Henry reached to sweep a dark tendril of hair from her eyes, and his fingertips lingered just a little too long on the soft curve of her cheek.

Everly took a tremulous inhale, and it was all Henry could do not to take her face in his hand and drag the pad of his thumb along the swell of her lower lip. So tempting…so perfectly pink.

"What do you mean?" she whispered as the dog's little ribcage began to rise and fall in a sleepy rhythm.

Henry felt his face crack into a grin. "Motherhood suits you, that's what I mean."

Everly's face went as white as a wedding dress. "W-what did you just say?"

"I said motherhood looks good on you. You've been a dog mom for less than an hour, but you and Holly already look like you've known each other for years." It was true. Everly and that dog were a match made in heaven. "You're a natural."

"The dog." Everly nodded and let out a quiet laugh, but the intimacy that had just wrapped around them like a blanket fell away. The loss seemed more painful than it should have. Henry was losing her again. She was closing herself off, and he had no idea why. "Of course."

"What did you think I meant, silly?" He gave her another affectionate knee bump, but this time she didn't reciprocate.

She cleared her throat. "I don't know. I think I'm just tired. It's been kind of a long day, and I just realized I still have to write my story."

Henry winced. "Ouch."

"Ouch is right. Writing this thing is going to be beyond awkward." Everly shifted so Holly slid out of her lap and curled into a sleepy ball against Henry's thigh. Then Everly stood and twisted her hair into a messy bun while she glanced around for her laptop.

The dog was awfully cute. Henry couldn't help but tuck her closer. "Do you want some help? We could write it together, like we used to do for the college paper."

"It's only two hundred fifty words. If I can't whip up a couple of cute paragraphs about a dog wedding on my own, then I *deserve* to lose my job. Thank you, though." She smiled down at him, and something about her gaze went bittersweet. "You know what?"

"Hmm?" Henry arched a brow as he ran a hand absently over Holly's soft pink belly.

"Parenthood looks pretty good on you, too."

Chapter Ten

Everly woke up slowly the next morning, dragged to consciousness by a weight pressing down on her chest.

She'd adopted a dog. As if it wasn't enough to be pregnant with a secret baby, she'd gone and added a frou-frou, needy little spaniel to the mix.

Everly didn't know the first thing about owning a dog. What was she supposed to do with Holly Golightly while she was at work? Everly was already on shaky ground at *Veil*. How was she going to dart out of the office to come home and take Holly for a walk while Colette had her going to dog weddings and writing about mundane things like tuxedo shoes?

Seriously, tuxedo shoes. The email about that assignment had come in late last night. Everly had done a cursory Google search before she'd gone to bed, and every pair looked the same. How many ways were there to reinvent a black patent loafer?

Everly slung her arm over her closed eyes and groaned. The collective weight of all her recent questionable choices was so heavy that she could barely breathe. A dog…what had she been thinking?

Then she opened her eyes and realized the heaviness bearing down on her was more than metaphorical. It was physical, as well—and it took the form of a furry little Cavalier with big, bright eyes and a merry, wagging tail. The dog was sprawled across Everly's chest, her tiny face mere inches from Everly's own.

Everly couldn't help but smile.

"Good morning," she said, prompting Holly to lick her cheek. "We might need to have a discussion about sleeping arrangements. You realize there are miles of prime mattress real estate freely available, don't you?"

She patted the empty space beside her, but Holly didn't budge. Everly could not keep sleeping with a dog lying on top of her, but her heart gave a little twist all the same. The dog needed her. And strangely enough, Everly needed Holly right back.

"We're a fine pair, aren't we?" she said, stroking the dog's silky fur. "Both jilted by our grooms at the altar."

At least Gregory hadn't tried to bite me. Still, the wounds from Everly's wedding day cut deep—so deep that she couldn't conceive of ever making the walk down the aisle again.

No, thank you. She'd experienced enough abandonment for a lifetime.

"Come on, little one. It's time to get up," Everly said, and Holly leapt off of her chest and commenced with spinning in rapid circles on the bed.

Clearly the Cavalier was a morning person. Or, er, morning dog. While Everly slipped her arms into her blue silk bathrobe, Holly grabbed hold of its sash with her teeth. An adorable game of tug-of-war ensued. Although, how Everly was going to manage this sort of morning chaos once she had a baby to take care of remained a mystery.

She pried the sash from Holly's teeth, scooped the pup into her arms and headed toward the kitchen. She needed coffee—immediately, even if all she could have was decaf.

Everly tiptoed out of her bedroom, hoping against hope that Henry was still asleep in the guest room. Last night had been a near miss. He'd come to her rescue yesterday, and when he'd held her hand on the sofa and said he'd always be there for her, all she could see when she looked at him was a knight in shining armor. Not a friend, not a confidante, but a partner. A lover. Maybe even a soulmate.

This is how true love is supposed to feel, she'd thought. Not like whatever she'd had with Gregory.

Then she'd blinked hard and forced herself to come to her senses. Henry was Henry. He was her friend, period. She was letting the fact that they were having a baby together go to her head. Their entire relationship felt so…confusing. Every little thing he did made her swoon, and it was really getting out of hand. If Everly hadn't had to write the dog wedding article last night, she might have stayed right there on the sofa and kissed him. The thought had certainly crossed her mind.

Quite a few times.

Everly pressed her cheek against Holly's warm form. "I'm a mess, sweet girl."

"That makes one of us."

Henry's words came from behind her, making her jump. Everly thought she'd been in the clear, but no. He must've opened the door to his room right after she'd passed it.

Her heart beat hard in response to the deep timbre of his voice. Her stupid, stupid heart.

"Just what is that supposed to mean? You forget that I'm well acquainted with your bedhead," Everly said as she braced herself to turn around and face him. "You're as much of a mess in the mornings as I…"

Her voice drifted off the minute she caught sight of him. All she could do was stop and stare.

"You were saying?" Henry shot her a ridiculously come hither look that reminded her of the time he'd gone to a college Halloween party dressed as James Bond.

Back then, he'd worn the same off-the-rack suit

he'd bought for his Columbia entrance interview. If not for the plastic martini glass in one hand and the water pistol in his other, he probably wouldn't have passed as 007. This morning was a decidedly different story.

"You're wearing a tuxedo," Everly said, mouth going instantly dry. "At seven in the morning."

She blinked. What was going on? Henry looked like he'd been visited by the Armani fairy overnight. The garment had clearly been made for him. It fit him like a glove, and the tailoring was impeccable—from Henry's perfect shoulders all the way down to his feet, where the slim-cut pants just barely rested atop his patent leather shoes. Alas, she was going to have to rethink her position on tuxedo shoes. They didn't look a bit boring on Henry.

Everly looked him up and down. Once, twice, three times, gaze lingering on his broad chest. He cleared his throat, and she forced herself to meet his gaze. Henry's eyes danced, and he flashed her a lopsided smile.

"Colette had the tux sent over this morning, so I was just trying it on. It's for the photo shoot *Veil* is doing to accompany my interview." No wonder the tux looked like it was made for him. The suit was bespoke. "Something about the way you're looking at me makes me think you approve?"

He came closer, and with each step he took toward her, Everly's heart thumped harder. Holly squirmed to get down, so Everly let the dog loose on the ground. When she stood back up, Henry was so close that she could see little flecks of gold in his blue irises, shining like hidden treasure.

He was the treasure, though, wasn't he? He always had been, right there under her nose, waiting for her to finally open her eyes and see the magic that had been right in front of her all along.

"You look like…" *A groom.* Everly's breath caught in her throat. Since when had she stopped seeing her man of honor when she looked at Henry? It wasn't as if she'd never seen her best friend in a tux before. She'd seen Henry in formal wear plenty of times, most notably on her wedding day and the notorious morning after.

But now when she looked at him, all she could imagine was another wedding day…a perfect one, with Henry waiting for her at the altar, looking exactly as he did at this moment. How quickly she seemed to forget the humiliation of her first walk down the aisle while Henry was around.

"Don't leave me hanging, E. What is it that I look like?" He tilted his head, searching her gaze until she felt as sheer and diaphanous as a bridal veil. As if he could see straight through to her deepest desires— desires she wasn't even sure she understood yet.

"You look nice." She swallowed. "That's what I'm trying to say. Very, very nice."

"Nice, huh?" A knowing smile tugged at his lips. "I'll take it."

And then all of a sudden, his hands were sliding

along the silk covering her hips, pulling her closer until she was flush against him. He was so warm, so solid, so… Henry. She could no longer imagine a time when he hadn't been part of her life. Part of her heart. And now he was going to be part of her future in a way neither of them could've imagined all those years ago at college.

"E," he said in a ragged whisper as he balled a handful of her silk robe in his fist, as if fighting the urge to kiss her was almost too much for him to handle.

Do it. Her bottom lip slipped between her teeth. *Please.*

She couldn't fight it anymore. There was still so much to say, so much to figure out, but she was tired. Tired of holding it all together on her own. Tired of pretending she didn't want him…need him…love him.

Henry dipped his head until there was just a sliver of space between their lips. The push and pull was achingly exquisite, pooling in Everly with a heat that made her breathless.

I don't love him. I can't love him. This isn't love. It's not.

His lips brushed against hers, as light as a feather, and somehow it was still enough to make her head spin.

She squeezed her eyes closed tight.

Then, just as that most tender of touches turned into a kiss, Holly let out a sharp bark.

Everly's eyes flew open. Henry's brow furrowed, as if he'd just been jerked awake from a lovely dream.

What were they doing? This couldn't happen. Period. Everly could not go around kissing Henry Aston like their quaint little living arrangement was in any way real or permanent—especially not when she was keeping such a huge secret from him.

"I think the dog needs to go out," she said, somehow finding the ability to form words when she was still tingling all over from just a gentle touch of his lips.

"Right." Henry nodded and raked a hand through his hair, looking as dazed as Everly felt. "I'll take Holly for a walk around the block."

"In your tuxedo? It's going to look like a bachelor walk of shame." Everly laughed, but she felt more like crying and she wasn't even sure she knew why.

"I don't mind." He gave her another long look, and for a second, there was a sadness in his features that made her heart clench. "Anything for you, E."

He brushed his lips gently against her cheek, a heartbreaking substitution for the kiss she craved so badly—the kiss she in no way deserved. Then he clipped Holly's leash onto her collar and the door shut quietly behind them, leaving Everly to process what had nearly just happened.

She touched her fingertips to her cheek, right

where Henry had just pressed his lips. If she could just hold onto that kiss, maybe she could convince herself that everything would turn out okay.

Only kisses weren't something that could be grabbed hold of, and neither were secrets.

But both somehow had the power to change everything.

Chapter Eleven

"So let me get this straight." Addison narrowed her gaze at Everly over the top of her cocktail glass. "You and Henry adopted a dog together, and you *still* haven't told him you're pregnant."

Everly reached for her virgin wedding cake martini—essentially just pineapple juice with a dash of vanilla extract in a glass with a sugared rim—and took a sip. It was Thursday night, so of course the *Veil* girls were at Bloom. Unfortunately, a perfectly lovely Martini Night had somehow turned into an impromptu interrogation with Everly in the hot seat.

"We didn't adopt Holly together. Henry adopted her on my behalf," Everly said, which was the truth… mostly.

For the past four nights, Holly had either slept

at the foot of Everly's bed or, more often, tucked into the crook of Everly's elbow. The Cavalier followed Everly around the apartment like a furry little shadow everywhere she went. If Everly swept into the bathroom and shut the door behind her, Holly pawed at the closed door until she was let in.

Of course the dog fawned all over Henry, too, but that was beside the point.

Daphne gave a slight headshake. "I still don't understand how all of this went down."

"That makes two of us," Addison said, and they clinked their martini glasses in solidarity.

Everly squirmed on her barstool. She'd admittedly left out a few details surrounding Holly's adoption when she first told the girls she'd gotten a dog. Addison was Everly's sister, and they had a great relationship, but she was also Everly's boss. Everly had been skating on thin enough ice at work already without anyone at *Veil* knowing about her mini breakdown in Central Park while on assignment for the magazine.

Everly shrugged as nonchalantly as she possibly could. "We were at a dog wedding, and we ended up taking the bride home."

"As one does," Daphne deadpanned.

Addison aimed her most accusatory side-eye at Everly. "What was Henry even doing there? Weren't you there covering the event for *Veil*?"

"He just…turned up." Everly twirled the stem of her glass. The line of questioning was getting intense. Couldn't they talk about something else, like the fashion show Addison had attended earlier this afternoon? Or the fact that Daphne's pink highlighted hair was now glittering with tiny little rhinestones? Since when had bedazzlers for hair become a thing? "Besides, Colette loved my story. She's actually letting me cover an event at Tiffany's tomorrow. I must be doing something right."

Finally.

In the four days since the dog wedding, Everly had done her best to act like a model employee. She'd labored over the two hundred fifty words on the dog story longer than she usually spent on an entire column. She made dog puns and gushed about the decor. She crammed more sheer romantic optimism into that piece than she had in all her columns for the past year combined. The end result had sounded like a rom-com on steroids, starring dogs instead of humans. Utterly ridiculous.

Colette had eaten it up with a spoon.

And now Everly was being rewarded for her efforts. Not *completely*—she still wasn't allowed to go anywhere near her column, but covering an event at Tiffany's was definitely a step in the right direction. Everly could hardly believe her luck, especially since she still hadn't managed to tell Henry about the baby.

She deserved some sort of cosmic punishment for keeping such an enormous secret, not an afternoon of walking a Tiffany-blue carpet at her favorite spot in all of Manhattan.

"It still seems odd that he was even there, but whatever." Addison shook her head and sipped her drink. "Face it, Sis. You and Henry are co-parenting that dog. You're practically playing house with the man, and for some crazy reason, you still can't bring yourself to tell him you're having his baby."

"I just haven't found the right time," Everly said.

"He's been here for *six* days," Addison countered.

"Not to mention the fact that he clearly worships the ground you walk on," Daphne said.

"No, he doesn't." Everly shook her head. "We're only friends, just like always."

She waited a beat for a bolt of lightning to appear out of nowhere and strike her dead. Shockingly, none materialized.

Her relationship with Henry had definitely changed since that night at the Plaza. As much as Everly liked to pretend otherwise, it had. She could no longer look at Henry without going weak in the knees, and the addition of a pajama shirt had done nothing to lessen his appeal. But it wasn't his body that she wanted so much as his heart. His lovely, lovely heart.

Addison gave her a beseeching look. "What are you so afraid of?"

Loving him. Everly swallowed. *Loving him and losing him.*

"I have my first prenatal doctor's appointment tomorrow morning, before the Tiffany's event. I'm going to tell him afterward so I can give him all the facts at once—due date and everything." Everly nodded and tried to look more confident than she actually felt.

"That sounds like procrastination," Addison said.

Shame spiraled through Everly. She wasn't this girl. She didn't keep secrets from people—especially not her best friend. Henry was usually the first person she trusted with her heart. Most often, he was the *only* person. "Telling him about the baby is going to change everything. You know it will. We'll never be the same, and I'm just not ready."

She wanted to hold on to what they had as long as she possibly could. The invisible line between friendship and love was growing thinner and thinner by the day. She and Henry were going through the motions, doing all the things they'd always done as friends. But every so often—like when Henry told her that motherhood suited her or when he made her breakfast or helped her slide her stilettos off her feet and gave her a foot rub at the end of the day—Everly caught a glimpse of what life could be like if she gave in and fully let herself step over that delicate line. The fullness of it, the potential of what they could be together, scared the life out of her. There was a danger in wanting something so bad that it hurt.

Once she held Henry Aston's heart in her hands, she'd never be able to let it go.

Friendship, she could handle. Anything more had the potential to leave her a brokenhearted mess on the bathroom floor. If she'd been bereft after losing Gregory, how would she ever handle the staggering loss of her best friend in the world?

The answer was plain and simple: she wouldn't handle it. *Couldn't.* Losing Henry would leave her damaged beyond all repair.

She leveled her gaze at Addison and Daphne. "Do either of you have any idea why Henry travels so much?"

Daphne shrugged one shoulder. "Because it's his job, right?"

"Right, but do you know why he took the job at *Wanderlust* in the first place?" Everly's grip tightened on her martini glass. She reminded herself to breathe before she accidentally snapped it in two. "Henry's father's dying wish was for him to see the world. His dad ran a bodega in Brooklyn for his entire adult life and dreamed of visiting all fifty states after he retired. Henry said the walls of his dad's home office were plastered with maps carefully highlighted with driving routes and pierced with red thumbtacks at all the places he wanted to stop and visit."

"Wow." Daphne's brows lifted. "Like father, like son."

"Henry was very close with his dad, and then when Henry was in high school, his father got sick. He passed away without ever leaving the state of New York," Everly said.

Daphne blew out a breath. "So that's why Henry is so set on visiting all seven continents."

Addison frowned. "I can't believe I've never heard this story before."

Everly shook her head. "He doesn't talk about it much, but that old, beat-up watch he always wears? His dad gave it to him. It has a Tolkien quote on the reverse side."

"Okay, that's pretty significant." Addison nodded. "How many continents has he seen so far? He's got to be close to hitting them all, right?"

Everly held up a single jazz hand. "Five down, two to go."

"Hon, people with babies travel," Daphne said.

"Not like Henry does." Everly shook her head. "It's his purpose. He lives for adventure, and once I tell him about the baby, I'm afraid he's going to look at me like we're an anchor around his neck."

Tears stung the backs of her eyes, and her breath came hard and fast. Never once had she let herself fully think about the exact nature of her darkest fears surrounding Henry, much less utter them out loud. Now that she had, it felt like she'd lifted the lid on Pandora's Box.

It wasn't pretty. Everly had every reason in the

world to trust Henry, and she did. But a tiny part of her—the fracture that had formed in her heart back when her dad passed away so unexpectedly—was a constant reminder that life was anything but predictable. People died. People left. They just disappeared sometimes, never to be seen again.

No amount of planning or caution could prepare you for it, especially when it happened clear out of the blue. Being abandoned in the middle of her wedding had ultimately been the best thing that could've happened to Everly, but it was still hard. It still hurt. And it had been like ripping the scab off the wounds of her past.

She wanted Henry. She wanted him so badly that she was incapable of rational thought when it came to their future…their *child*. She might even love him.

If only she'd let herself.

"Henry would never think that," Addison said. "Never."

"In my head, I know you're right. But my heart is another story," Everly conceded. "It's not just that, though. Anything could happen to Henry. He could go away on a trip and be trampled by elephants. Or eaten by a lion. Or attacked by a penguin."

Addison's martini glass paused en route to her lips. Her forehead puckered. "Did you just say 'penguin'?"

Everly sniffed, but the tears were flowing freely now. Now that she'd finally let them fall, there was no stopping them. "It's rare, but it happens—I looked it up. Did you know that penguins have a curved beak that can pierce a person's skin? And Antarctica is one of the continents Henry still hasn't crossed off his list."

Daphne reached over to dab Everly's wet cheeks with a cocktail napkin. "Hon, you're spiraling. Henry definitely isn't going to be the victim of a random penguin attack."

"You have no idea how badly I want to believe you." Everly took a shuddering breath and balled the damp cocktail napkin in her fist as Ron, the bartender, placed another virgin wedding cake martini in front of her.

He shot her a sympathetic smile before he left.

"We might need to find another happy hour spot." Everly sighed and took a giant sip of her drink. "Every time I come here lately, I seem to fall apart."

More likely, she'd been on a continual downward trajectory since her nonwedding. She shuddered to think about what might happen when she reached rock bottom.

Addison leaned back on her barstool. "Bite your tongue. Do you really think there's another bar out there somewhere that would invent a cocktail just for us?"

She had a point.

"Back to the matter at hand, though—Daphne is right. There's not a penguin on this earth who would attack Henry." Addison set her palms down flat on the table. "But he could just as easily get hit by a cab crossing the street right here in Manhattan as he could get eaten by a lion. Actually, the cab scenario seems far more likely. Statistically speaking and all."

The pineapple juice in Everly's drink seemed too sticky and sweet all of a sudden. She set her glass down. "Not helpful."

"I'm not trying to freak you out, but you can't push Henry away just because you're afraid of what might happen—that he might leave for some far off land or fall victim to a rogue puffin." Addison waved a hand, presumably encompassing the far ends of the earth and all the places where Henry's passport still hadn't been stamped.

"Penguin," Everly said. "There's a difference. Puffins are quite placid."

Daphne fiddled with one of her earrings. "Is this sudden expertise in wildlife a pregnancy thing? I hope so. It seems much more fun than morning sickness."

"We're getting way off track." Addison reached for her glass and used it to gesture toward Everly. "The point is that you can't keep living like this. I know it's hard, but are you planning on emotionally shutting out every man who ever loves you?"

Maybe...

Probably.

Yes.

Everly's heart wrenched.

"Because that's no way to live, and I know it's not what you want for your baby. I know you, Ev. You're going to love that child with every last bit of your soul, and if you gave a Henry a real chance, you'd love him the same way." Addison's expression went tender. "Something tells me you already do."

Everly couldn't handle looking her sister in the eye anymore, so she dropped her gaze to the glossy high-top table. She stared so long and hard at its smooth wooden surface that her vision went blurry.

Addison cleared her throat. "But first, you really need to tell him about the baby."

When Everly got home from Bloom, she was startled to be greeted by complete and total silence when she opened the door to the apartment. Holly usually welcomed her the second she crossed the threshold with a wag of her entire backside, not just her merry feathered tail.

Not so, tonight. The pup was conspicuously absent. The apartment lights were off, with just a pale lavender glow coming from the living room.

Everly dropped her handbag and keys on the foyer table and tiptoed toward the quiet hum of a television turned down low. When she reached the archway with heavy crown molding that led to the living room, she paused for a beat to take in a sight that tugged on her heartstrings until she felt feather-light inside...filled with a hope that had seemed so elusive to her just an hour ago when she'd poured her heart out to Addison and Daphne.

Henry lay sprawled on her sofa with one arm slung over his head and the other dangling off the edge of the tufted velvet fabric. Once again, the pajama bottoms that had become Everly's nemesis were slung low on his hips. The newly acquired pajama shirt? Nowhere to be seen. An old episode of *Friends* flickered on the flat-screen while Henry slept. It was one of Everly's favorites—the installment where Monica, Phoebe and Rachel all hang out in wedding dresses for an entire night, eating popcorn and watching television. Henry always said the scene reminded him of Everly and her *Veil* girls.

Everly stood watching the shadows dance over Henry's bare chest and the chiseled planes of his face. She knew that face so well, could trace every tiny scar, every familiar feature—even though it was the face of a grown man now, not the college boy who'd become her salvation during the darkest days she'd ever known.

He was so beautiful, inside and out. Everly's knees turned to water. She couldn't take her eyes off him.

Henry's sooty black eyelashes drifted open, as if he could feel her gaze traveling slowly down the length of his body—so new to her and yet so familiar at the same time. Everly had always heard about a thing called muscle memory, a process where your body learned things over time by repetition. Well, her heart was a muscle, wasn't it? It was no wonder that she and Henry were such a natural fit. The intimacy they'd found that night at the Plaza had been years in the making, built on a connection they'd formed and nurtured over time. The pull that she felt toward him was real and raw, every bit as physical as it was emotional.

Her heart *knew* Henry. He was a part of her and always would be, no matter what happened in the days, weeks and years to come.

Their eyes met in the darkened room. For a long moment, neither of them said anything. Henry's deep blue irises seemed almost bottomless, as if their capacity to see her—*really* see her—was infinite. Timeless.

Warmth spread through Everly as his lips curved into a drowsy smile. He shifted so he was sitting up with his long legs stretched out in front of him, and then he patted the empty cushion beside him.

"We'll never both fit lengthwise on that thing," she said, even as she walked toward the sofa, drawn toward him like a moth to a dangerous, dazzling flame.

"Sure we will," he said. His voice dipped low—so low that it tickled her insides. "But we have to keep quiet."

He pressed a finger to his lips and cut his gaze to the space beneath the coffee table, where Holly was curled into a tight little ball on top of a lump of fabric.

"Is that—?" Everly whispered as she sat down beside Henry and studied the dog's tiny body, eyes closed, nose tucked gently under her tail.

"My pajama top?" A dimple flashed in Henry's left cheek. "Yes. I know this is a no nudity zone, but she kept darting to the front door every time she heard a noise outside, pining for you to come home. I think she might have separation anxiety."

Everly could relate. She was suffering from the same affliction, and the object of her desire hadn't even left the country. Yet.

Henry murmured, voice dropping even lower, "I've told you about Peaches before, right?"

Everly nodded. "The golden retriever your family had when you were a kid."

"She used to like sleeping in the dirty laundry basket. It was her favorite spot. Dad always said it was because the clothes we wore smelled like us and Peaches found the scent comforting. I thought I'd give it a try."

Everly's gaze flitted toward the Cavalier sleeping soundly on top of his pajama shirt. Henry had made a little nest out of it for the dog that reminded Everly of the circular swirl of a Christmas tree skirt. Holly's paws twitched ever so slightly, like she was far off in dreamland, chasing rabbits.

"Looks like it worked," Henry said quietly.

"It sounds like someone missed me," Everly whispered, happiness sparkling inside of her as she regarded Holly. If she'd had to, she'd break up that dog wedding all over again, even if it meant losing her job the second time around.

Henry reached up to cup Everly's cheek, gently forcing her gaze back to him. "We both missed you."

Her heart was aflame now, burning as swiftly and easily as a sheet of paper freshly struck by a match. If Everly wasn't careful, it would be reduced to a pile of ash by sunrise the next morning.

Even so, she craved the burn. Wanted it…needed it. Needed *him*. The time for caution had been weeks ago, before she'd opened the door to the honeymoon suite and welcomed Henry inside. If she'd known then what she did now, would she have still answered his knock? Would she have leaned in and kissed him, begged him to lay her down on that big, soft bed, if she'd known they were about to create a child together…a life?

Yes, her soul whispered. Because this was the life she wanted most of all. Not a safe, guarded existence, but a *life*. Love. A family—one she'd created with the man who'd always held her heart.

"I haven't been gone long enough for you to miss me," she said and somehow her fingertips made their way to his warm, hard chest. A tiny groan escaped him at the first hesitant moment of contact, and a shiver rippled through Everly. Then she peered up at him through the thick fringe of her eyelashes— gaze full of questions as she let her fingertips dance lower, and lower still, perilously close to the waist-band of those maddening pajama pants.

Henry's response was a tortured whisper. "Don't you know by now, darling? I always miss you. I've been missing you for as long as I can remember."

"I'm right here," she said, leaning down until her lips were just a whisper away from his.

"Thank God," Henry breathed. His breath fanned over her face, warm and welcoming.

What was *happening*? They weren't supposed to be doing this again. When she'd left Bloom, Everly had headed home with every intention of telling Henry about the baby, and now every part of her body ached with need. They were barreling toward a flagrant violation of the aforementioned no nudity rule—a violation of the most dire sort.

But Everly suddenly didn't care at all. Who'd ever decided that pajama shirts were a good idea in the first place?

Her hair fell around them in a dark curtain, shut-ting out the light…shutting out everything so that it was just the two of them. Them and the overwhelm-ing yearning that was always there, stretching be-tween them like a smooth satin ribbon. Henry's hands slid over her back, leaving a trail of goose bumps in their wake and the satin ribbon pulled unbearably taut.

"There's something I need to tell you," she said, breathless.

Henry tilted his face toward hers so their lips met.

"Is it important?" he murmured against her mouth, and it was as if he'd plucked the string on a violin. Every syllable reverberated through her, humming with warmth, electricity and sweet, sweet music.

She couldn't take it anymore—the memories, the yearning, the closeness.

Is it important?

Everly kissed him, and it felt like a lifetime had passed since their lips last met. So much had happened since that first kiss seven weeks ago, but as Henry's mouth moved against hers and his hands buried themselves in her hair, she was transported right back to the beginning—back to the day they'd first met. When her lashes drifted shut, years upon years of friendship flickered behind her eyes like a movie. She and Henry holding hands as they tossed their college graduation caps in the air. Hugging goodbye at the airport when Henry left for London. Visits from far-off places and the way they always fit back together like two puzzle pieces, no matter how much time they'd spent apart.

Before she even got to the scene from the Plaza

Hotel, Everly recognized the dreamlike film reel in her head for what it truly was—a love story.

Is it important?

Everly tried to grab hold of Henry's question, but it slipped through her fingers as she fell deeper and deeper into his kiss. She didn't want it to end. Not now...not yet.

Henry, my love. It's the most important thing of all.

He pulled back slightly, brushed the hair from her face and smiled at her with stars in his eyes. A whole galaxy right there in the bottomless blue. "You're here. You're really here with me, aren't you? These past six days, I've felt like you've been holding part of yourself back, but you're here now."

"I am." She nodded, smiling so hard that it hurt. Or maybe the ache in her chest was the secret she still kept, threatening to tear everything apart.

"Can we wait and talk later?" Henry cupped her face in both his hands, ran his thumb against her bottom lip, already bee-stung and tender from his kisses. "Tonight, I just want to touch you...love you. Will you let me do that, darling? Just for us this time. Not to make you forget anyone else or to remind yourself that you're desirable. Because you are, E. *I* desire you. Always have, always will."

Always...

Everly held on to that word with all of her might. She knew he hadn't meant it as a vow, but she pretended he had as she pressed it to her heart and nodded. "Yes. Yes, please. We can talk later."

One more day, that's all…just one more.

What could it hurt?

Chapter Twelve

The second Henry opened his eyes the following morning, relief flowed through him at the realization that he wasn't in for a repeat of the torturous morning-after from the Plaza. Everly's graceful legs were still entwined with his, soft rays of sunshine streamed through the window, and pink cherry blossoms danced against the glass.

Outside, yellow taxicabs honked while commuters poured onto the city sidewalks, the subway rumbled underfoot and hot steam rose from manhole covers. Manhattan was already alive and thrumming, but all of that felt absurdly far away when Everly's head rested on his chest, hair fanned around her face like a dark halo. They may as well have been waking up in a hillside bungalow in Antigua with palm trees swaying overhead and bougainvillea growing wild along the rambling path to the sea.

Henry took a relaxing inhale and ran a lazy finger along the curve of Everly's hip. At long last, all felt right in their little world.

"Mmm." Everly stirred against him, purring like a kitten. "Morning."

Henry pressed a kiss to her hair. "Morning, sunshine."

"You sound perfectly alert. How long have you been lying here awake?" She shifted so she could rest her chin on her hands planted in the center of his chest and grinned up at him.

The Plaza Hotel may as well have been on an entirely different continent instead of the other side of the park.

"Not long." He twirled a lock of hair around one of his fingertips. "Barely enough time to think about whisking you away to Antigua."

"Antigua." Everly blinked—not quite the reaction he'd expected. "That sounds…"

Henry arched a brow. "Romantic?"

She bit her lip. "Very."

"Good. I'm including it as the top spot in the *Veil* honeymoon feature," he said.

"Oh, so this Antigua business is about work." She looked almost relieved, as if he'd expected her to get right out of bed and pack a suitcase.

The thought wasn't without its appeal. In all the

years he and Everly had known each other, they'd never been on an extended trip out of the country together. They'd spent a summer at a Hamptons share house, but that had been ages ago. She'd come to Europe a few times for the Wolf Granger Awards. Before Gregory had come along, she'd spent her vacation days with Henry in London, and he'd taken her to dinner in a glass igloo overlooking the Thames, to afternoon tea in the gardens at Kensington Palace and for a private behind-the-scenes tour of a royal jewelry exhibit at Sotheby's, where she'd gotten to try on a priceless tiara that once belonged to Princess Margaret.

But London was home for Henry. He wanted to show Everly some of the places he'd seen on his travels. He wanted to kiss her under a waterfall in Zambia. He wanted to skinny dip with her on the Amalfi Coast, drunk on moonlight and fine red wine. He wanted to press his lips to her bare shoulder while the sun dipped low beneath the whitewashed villages of Santorini.

But those things could wait. Everly wanted to get her career back on track, and Henry was a patient man. They'd waited this long to be together. There was no rush.

Henry pressed a finger to the worried crease lining her forehead. "Relax, darling. It was just a daydream. I know you and the girls have big plans at

Veil. We have all the time in the world to go places together."

She sat up and ran a hand through her tumbling hair. "Right. So much time."

Henry's heart gave a little twinge. For a second, he could almost feel her slipping away again. He braced himself for the far-off look to come back to her violet eyes, but then she met his gaze again. Gave him a smile so tender it took his breath away.

Then there was no more worry, no more daydreaming, no more talk. There were just soft sighs, kisses and a connection that went beyond words as they made love again. Slow and easy this time, like the calm before a storm.

"I almost forgot," Henry said, tucking a lock of hair behind Everly's ear as she emerged from the bedroom donning a hot pink dress with a taffeta bodice and a full tulle ballerina-length skirt with an empire waist sash that tied in a stiff pink bow.

Choosing something to wear to the Tiffany's event had been a challenge. Her tiny hint of a baby bump seemed to be expanding at an exponential rate all of a sudden. Everything in her closet with a fitted waist was just a little too snug. Yet another reason why she needed to tell Henry she was pregnant. She wouldn't be able to hide it forever.

And she didn't *want* to hide it—not anymore. After last night, the secret felt like a time bomb, tick-tick-ticking away, loud and terrible, just waiting to explode right in her face. While Henry had been thinking about Antigua, her mind had been drifting to things like cribs and strollers and family Christmas cards.

"Forgot what?" she said, reaching to adjust the collar of his dress shirt for him. Holly stretched out beside them on the floor with a twisted chew stick propped between her paws.

"You said you wanted to talk to me about something." Henry's gaze swept her up and down, and his lips curved into an appreciative smile. "You look amazing, by the way. Going somewhere special today, E?"

She toyed with the charm on her necklace, a nervous habit that had begun to spin out of control. "Thank you. I have a…meeting…this morning, and then I'm attending a private viewing party at Tiffany's. Colette asked me to cover it for the digital site. Can you believe it?"

"You? At Tiffany's? Why, yes. Yes, I can." He gave her chin a gentle tap upward and pressed a tender kiss to her lips. "I wish I could be there. It would really be something to see my girl in her natural habitat."

His girl. Butterflies took flight in Everly's belly. *His*.

"Come. I'm sure I can get you on the list. We can check out the diamonds and then go for a walk, find a nice shady spot in the park and have that chat I mentioned." Everly took a deep breath. This was it. No more waiting, no more putting off the inevitable.

"You want to go for a walk in the park?" Henry cast an amused look at her feet. "In those shoes?"

Everly glanced down at her glittery gold Kate Spade mules. The heel was a round acrylic snow globe with a tiny porcelain wedding cake inside. All the *Veil* girls had bought a pair the very same day Addison first spotted them at Bloomingdale's.

"What else would I wear to an event at Tiffany's?" She flashed him a little foot pop to showcase the shoe's light blue sole—a dead ringer for the same shade as the jewelry store's legendary little blue boxes.

"Point taken. Audrey Hepburn would be proud." Henry winked. "So it's a date, then—our first official one. How does that sound?"

Everly felt her smile go wobbly around the edges. *You're going to be a dad!* That was normal first date conversation, wasn't it? "Perfect."

Then she rose up on tiptoe to wind her arms around his neck and give him a goodbye kiss before she headed to her doctor's appointment. It was all going to be okay. It had to. Joy bubbled up in her, and for a moment she thought maybe she should just go ahead and tell Henry about the baby right then and there.

Why wait another second? Maybe once he'd gotten over the shock he could even come with her to her doctor's appointment.

She squeezed her eyes closed as his arms held her tight, pressing her against him, heart to heart. She took the deepest of deep breaths, and as the embrace ended, she said. "Actually…"

Her eyes fluttered open, and then her words ground to an immediate halt as she spied a slick brochure sitting on the kitchen counter next to the espresso machine.

"E? You okay?" Henry gave the sash on her dress a little tug, just like he had on her wedding night. Such a sweet, innocent gesture, but the mirrored nature of it nearly made her cry.

"Fine. Just curious, though." She pointed at the brochure. "What's that?"

Everly's stomach lurched. She couldn't stop staring at the cover shot of a glacier so intensely blue and barren that it looked like a cut aquamarine stone sitting all by itself on a velvet jeweler's tray. A banner across the top screamed *Welcome to Antarctica*, and to her complete and utter horror, a group of penguins dotted the landscape. Hundreds and hundreds of them, jet black against the cool blue snow.

Everly's gaze bore into the photograph until the birds began to look like a flock of well-dressed undertakers.

"Oh, that." Henry lifted his shoulder in a half shrug, oblivious to the riot going on inside her. "*Wan-*

derlust sent it over yesterday via overnight delivery. They want to send me to Antarctica once my work is done on the June issue for *Veil*."

"Antarctica." Everly crossed her arms and then promptly uncrossed them. She couldn't seem to figure out what to do with her limbs. Or her face. It took superhuman effort just to remember to blink. "Wow, your sixth continent. You must be excited."

"Yes and no." His gaze shifted toward Holly, prancing around the apartment in search of a hiding place for what was left of her chew stick. "I haven't decided if I'm going yet or not."

Everly's spirits lifted a fraction of an inch. A millimeter, at best. "Why not?"

"It would be quite an extended trip, and they want me to go by boat so I can write about what it's like to cross the Drake Passage." He massaged the back of his neck. "It's a lot to think about."

Everly nodded dumbly. She'd heard about the Drake Passage, and it definitely sounded more dangerous than a casual run-in with a penguin. He hadn't agreed to go, though. His answer hadn't been an automatic yes, even though it would have ticked off the next to last continent on his list.

He didn't say no, either.

"How long?" she asked, trying—and failing—to keep the telltale hitch out of her voice.

Henry answered without preamble. "Six months."

All the air left Everly's lungs in a sudden, petrifying whoosh.

Six months.

Six months?

That was half a year. It was also *two-thirds* of a pregnancy. She could possibly even give birth while he was still there cavorting with the evil penguins.

"You look worried." Henry reached for her hand and gave her fingertips a playful tug. "Don't be. It's just another assignment—one I doubt that I'll even take."

But if he didn't take this assignment, another one would come along right after it. This was Henry's life. It's what he did.

Everly nodded and somehow forced her lips into a smile. She was being unfair, and she knew it. Once he knew about the baby, Henry would have all the facts and could make up his mind accordingly.

She just wished she would've listened to Addison and Daphne and told him right away before the situation had gotten so complicated. Before Antarctica and the penguins.

Before she'd gone and let herself come so dangerously close to falling for him.

"I should go. I have that meeting to get to." Everly's voice sounded overly cheerful, borderline manic. She needed to get out of there. Now.

She bent down to bury her face in Holly's fur and tell the dog goodbye, pausing to try and get herself together. *Just breathe. You can fall apart once you've left the building.* This was New York. People cried on sidewalks, subways, trains and everything in between. No one would bat an eye at a pregnant woman sobbing in her fabulous shoes.

Everly wished with all her might that she could call an emergency fashion closet meeting so the girls could talk some sense into her. It was too late, though. It was too late for a lot of things, like being honest and up front with Henry right away. And protecting her heart by not jumping into bed with him… twice.

She stood and smoothed down the bright pink tulle of her dress. If she didn't leave right now, she'd be late for her appointment at the obstetrician's office.

"See you at Tiffany's?" Henry asked, affection glowing in his eyes.

Longing whispered through her. Even when she was half terrified of what might happen between them, even when Henry had one foot in Antarctica or some other place on the far side of the globe, even when the thought of losing him nearly dragged her to her knees…he was always her favorite person. Always the one she wanted.

Everly nodded. "See you there."

Half an hour later, Everly sat in her obstetrician's office filling out a stack of forms about her medical history and feeling acutely alone.

She was the only patient in the waiting room who wasn't accompanied by a partner. Women in various stages of pregnancy occupied the seats around her, and not one of them sat all by themselves. Everly wished she would've asked Addison or Daphne to come with her.

Her throat clogged as she finished filling out the paperwork and handed it to the woman dressed in scrubs with a pastel baby rattle print sitting at the front desk. Henry should have been there with Everly, not Addison or Daphne. He was the father. Coming here all by herself didn't just make her feel lonely; it also felt like a betrayal of sorts.

How have I let this secret go so far?

She reminded herself that she was still in her first trimester. It wasn't like she was about to give birth any second, and she'd tried to tell him about the baby—several times, in fact.

Including last night.

Warmth filled her chest every time she thought about the way Henry looked when she got home from Bloom, sleeping so peacefully on her sofa with Holly curled into a tiny ball on top of his shirt. The sight of him there—so handsome, so at home—had put such a pang in her heart that it had been easy to forget all the reasons they were better off as friends than lovers. Had she really thought she could keep Henry at arm's length, after everything that had happened since she'd been jilted at the altar? He was *Henry,* not some random one-night stand. He'd always felt like family to Everly. And now, at long last, they *were* family, tied to each other for life, whether or not she was ready to open herself up to that kind of vulnerability.

"From the look of things, you're almost two months along," the doctor said after Everly had been given a blood test and ushered into an exam room.

She nodded, arms wrapped around herself in the flimsy pink paper gown she'd been asked to change into. "Sounds right."

"That puts you due right around October 1." Dr. Calderon—a bright-eyed young woman with a high ponytail, a crisp white doctor's coat and two-tone ballerina flats—smiled kindly at her. "I have a few protocols I want to go over with you, we need to dis-cuss finding a good pediatrician, and then we can do a quick ultrasound to confirm the due date if that works for you?"

Everly nodded. "That sounds great."

She couldn't believe she needed to start looking for a pediatrician already. She probably needed to go ahead and start looking at preschools while she was at it. Her mind reeled. How could all this be happening so fast?

"First thing, we need to get you started on pre-natal vitamins right away. I'll leave a bottle for you up front and you can pick them up on your way out. Make sure you take them with food to avoid any nausea on top of whatever stomach upset you may be experiencing from morning sickness," Dr. Calderon said.

Everly rested her hand on her stomach. "I'll make sure and remember that."

The doctor went on to list a variety of tests Everly would need to assure that her pregnancy was proceeding without any complications, and then she offered her a pamphlet about prenatal nutrition and a month-to-month guide to fetal development. According to the chart, her baby was now approximately the size of a blueberry, which definitely didn't seem large enough to make Everly strain to get her high-waisted trousers and more fitted dresses buttoned. Then again, maybe Henry's delicious homemade pasta and all those wedding cake mocktails at Bloom were the real culprits in this particular scenario.

The next question Dr. Calderon asked Everly caught her a bit off guard. "Will the baby's father be present and supportive during your pregnancy?"

Everly had no idea how to respond. *Maybe...unless he decides to go live on a glacier for the next six months. Oh, and he'll also be commuting from London.*

"Um. The truth is, I haven't exactly told him I'm pregnant yet. He's my..." *Man of honor.* An image of Henry in his tuxedo, bow tie hanging loose around his collar, flashed in her mind. "...friend. My best friend, actually. Henry."

The doctor nodded. "I understand."

Did she? If so, Everly wished Dr. Calderon could explain it to her, because she was still trying to wrap her head—and her heart—around where she and Henry were supposed to go from here.

"I'm going to tell him today," Everly said.

Dr. Calderon smiled. "Good. I think you'll find that once the news about the baby is out in the open, you'll experience a lot less stress. Henry seems like an important person in your life. It will be nice to have his support over the course of the next seven months."

A bittersweetness settled over Everly. She didn't want to go through this alone, but didn't she want to keep Henry from pursuing his dreams, either. Her pregnancy had been a surprise all along, but things between her and Henry hadn't felt quite like such a no-win situation until right that second. "I'm sure you're correct."

"All right, then. Shall we proceed with the ultrasound?"

As instructed, Everly laid back on the exam table and placed her feet in the stirrups. A nurse entered the room and pushed a cart with a video monitor on it right next to the table. At first, all she could see were dark shadows moving across the screen accompanied by a swishing sound. The noise was strange and disorienting, like being at the bottom of a swimming pool.

Then a rapid thump-thump-thump sound filled the air, and Everly's eyes flooded with tears. "Is that the baby's heartbeat?"

Dr. Calderon grinned but kept her gaze glued to the video monitor. "It sure is. Sounds like you've got a strong, healthy baby growing in there."

Relief coursed through Everly. She hadn't even realized she'd been holding her breath until she let out a long exhale. She peered at the screen as a fuzzy white spot came into view in the dark center of the monitor.

She gasped. "And is that—?"

"Your baby?" The doctor's grin widened. "It sure is. Except..."

A furrow formed in Dr. Calderon's brow as she craned her neck and leaned in for a closer look at the monitor. She moved the ultrasound wand around, and the crease in her forehead grew deeper.

Everly could no longer look at the screen. She could barely make sense of the shadows moving across it, anyway. But the look on her doctor's face told her everything she needed to know—whatever she'd found on the ultrasound was *not* normal.

"What is it?" Everly asked as dread took hold of her. "Is everything okay?"

She sent up a silent prayer. *Please, please let it be okay.* She loved that little blueberry from the very depths of her soul. She'd never doubted that for a second.

Dr. Calderon's gaze moved from the screen to Everly, and the look of concern on her face melted into a smile.

"Don't worry, Everly. Everything is just fine with your pregnancy—doubly fine, as a matter of fact." She pointed to the monitor, where, just moments before, there had been one fuzzy white blob and now there were two. They looked like a pair of tiny bubbles, side by side. "But I hope you're up for another surprise, because you and your best friend Henry are having twins."

Chapter Thirteen

*T*wins.

Two babies.

Two tiny little blueberries who, months from now, would grow into newborn infants.

Everly's mind was a complete and total blur as she walked the Tiffany-blue carpet at the jewelry event. Her appointment at the obstetrician had taken far longer than she'd anticipated—mostly due to the stunning news that she was carrying twins—and she'd been forced to go directly to the flagship store on Fifth Avenue from Dr. Calderon's office. Do not pass Go. Do not collect two hundred dollars.

The flash of a camera burst nearby caused her to go momentarily blind. *Just smile. Pose for the photographers. Chin up, hand on hip, dazzling grin.*

You're thrilled to be here, remember? Everly had to give herself the pep talk to end all pep talks just to get to the end of the short carpet and through the front door.

Once inside, she paused for a beat near a glass case filled with sparkling gemstones and tried to get her bearings. She'd been elated when Colette had given her this assignment. She couldn't screw it up.

The event was an invitation-only party for members of the media, fashion elite and prominent New Yorkers to view the store's new line of engagement rings. The collection was inspired by the late Victorian era, with platinum settings decorated with fine lace-style filigree. Halos of tiny diamonds surrounded multicarat sparklers, and some of the rings even featured highly refined detailing shaped like bows, ribbons or crowns. The only photos Everly had seen ahead of the party had been three teaser images that the store released in tandem with the emailed invitations. She'd been looking forward to seeing the entire array of engagement rings—twenty new styles in all—ever since she'd first heard of the launch.

It all seemed so wholly unimportant at the moment, though. She was having a hard time concentrating on any one thing in front of her. So much sparkle…so much glitter. It was like staring directly into a disco ball. Her head spun, and she found herself wishing she'd taken a page out of Holly Golightly's book—the character, not the dog—and rolled up to the jewelry store in a pair of dark sunglasses with a Danish in her hand.

Her stomach growled. She was starving. Because she was apparently eating for *three* now.

"Hi there, gorgeous," someone behind her said.

Everly turned around, and her eyes nearly fell out of her head. "Henry."

She was so stunned to see him that she nearly asked what he was doing there, and then she remembered that she'd been the one who'd called and asked for his name to be added to the guest list. She'd made the call on the way to the doctor's office. This was supposed to be their first date, and she'd completely forgotten about it.

He tilted his head, lips curved into an amused half grin. "You seem surprised to see me."

"Not surprised." A lie. Super. Now she was lying right to his face in addition to keeping a whopper of a secret from him. Correction: two secrets. *Twin* secrets. "Just very happy to see you. You have no idea."

Henry's eyes crinkled as his face split into a wide grin. "Back at you, babe."

Babe, darling, gorgeous... Everly loved the endearments. They made her glow inside.

A waiter in black tie passed by carrying a tray of champagne flutes, and Henry snagged two of them.

He handed one of the crystal glasses to Everly and clinked his flute against hers. "Cheers to a first date nearly a decade in the making."

"I'll drink to that." Everly held the champagne to her lips to take a pretend sip, and the smell of the alcohol nearly made her blanch.

How was she ever going to get through this party? She wanted to tuck her arm through Henry's elbow and go straight to the park, where they could be alone.

"Shall we take a look at the jewels? They've got a few stations where you can take some of the rings for a spin." Henry slid his cell phone out of the inside pocket of his suit jacket. "I can snap photos of you trying them on for your article. It'll be like working together at the college paper all over again."

Except for the minor detail that they were now the parents of one needy Cavalier King Charles spaniel and the soon-to-be mom and dad to twin babies.

"That sounds like fun," Everly said, because after all, this party was a dream. It should have been, anyway. And if anything could take her mind off the bombshell she'd just gotten, it was this place, with this man.

They perused the new collection, and Henry seemed happy to hang back and let Everly take the spotlight, chatting with the jewelry designers and corporate executives who were delighted to have a reporter from *Veil* in attendance. When she tried on the showcase piece—a ten-carat emerald cut engagement ring with band comprised of the daintiest halo of diamonds that Everly had ever seen—Henry stepped forward and, with a wink, offered to slip it onto her finger.

Everly's heart pounded and her fingers trembled as he took her hand in his and slid the ring in place. It would have been so easy to believe that all of this was real, that they were just a regular couple trying on engagement rings at New York's most iconic jewelry store. *Too* easy, actually. And the way Henry's smile went tender as the diamond shimmered on her finger made Everly's heart turn over in her chest.

Maybe this could *be real*, she thought. It wasn't the craziest thing to believe, was it?

She returned the ring to the attendant and then smiled up at Henry.

"Let's get out of here," she whispered.

He placed his hand onto the small of her back and then slid it to the curve of her waist, pulling her close. "I thought you'd never ask," he murmured against her ear.

A shiver ran through her from head to toe, and for the life of her, Everly couldn't tell whether it was from excitement or panic.

There's nothing to be afraid of. She tried to swallow, but her throat had gone bone-dry. The party was over, quite literally speaking. They'd be at the park in a matter of minutes, and once she gave him the big news, everything would change.

For better or worse, as the saying went.

"Before we go, maybe you'd like to open this."

Henry slipped his free hand into his trouser pocket and pulled out one of the little blue boxes tied with a white satin bow that the store was so famous for.

Everly's mouth dropped open. "What is that, and where did it come from?"

"While you were busy working, I snuck off and picked it up on the third floor. Don't worry. It's just a little trinket," he said, as if the thought of a big diamond solitaire nestled inside the box was an idea too absurd to contemplate. Which it was. Of course it was. Reality check: she wasn't even sure if they were boyfriend-girlfriend now. He could up and leave for the South Pole on the next plane out of JFK. "And if you really want to know what it is, you should open it."

"Right now?"

"Why not? I happen to know you have no self-control whatsoever when it comes to opening gifts," he said.

She snatched the box from his hand. "I should've never told you about the time Addison and I opened all the gifts under the tree in the middle of the night a week before Christmas and then rewrapped them so our parents wouldn't know."

Henry arched a brow. "Classic Everly."

"I was *twelve*," she countered.

"And you apparently haven't changed a bit. I know for a fact that you snuck a peek inside your stocking on Christmas Eve that time you came to London for the holidays." He shot her a look, half accusatory, half amused. "I know you, E. You love getting gifts and you can't keep a secret to save your life."

Everly's grin froze in place. It was just playful banter, but the fact that he didn't know her quite as well as he thought he did struck her as profoundly sad.

It's just a tiny, blueberry-sized exception of a secret.

She gave the ribbon on the box a gentle tug, and the bow slowly came undone. "I'm going to open this now."

His eyes gleamed. "By all means, don't let me stop you."

She handed him the ribbon and lifted the lid from the box. A tiny blue felt bag was nestled inside on a bed of tissue paper. Everly had a strange feeling of déjà vu as she picked it up and spilled its contents into her palm.

A shiny silver initial charm fell into her hand. It matched the E charm Henry had given her for college graduation exactly—same size, same dainty script—only this one was an H.

"It's for Holly. I thought you might like it for her collar," he said. Then he scrunched his face as Everly looked at him with her heart in her throat. She adored the way he remembered things, the way her fondest and most memorable moments from their friendship seemed to be his favorite memories, too. "Is it too much?"

She shook her head.

"Not too much at all. It's just right. I love it."
Everly swallowed.

I love you.

No. That wasn't right. She wasn't supposed to be
in love with Henry. That thought had to have been the
double dose of pregnancy hormones talking. They
were best friends...who'd slept together twice and
were having twins.

Right, because that's totally a thing.

He reached out to touch a gentle finger to the E
charm resting in the dip between her collarbones.
"Have I mentioned how much I love it that you've
started wearing this again?"

"Not lately," Everly said through a shaky breath.
"I'm glad, though."

They were doing what they always did—tiptoeing
around the things they were both too afraid to say. At
least that's what it felt like. Everly couldn't bring herself to admit how she really felt about Henry, though.
If he didn't feel the same way, it would crush her.

"Are you sure you're okay? You don't seem quite
like yourself today. You're not going to faint again
on me, are you?" Henry eyed her with concern.

Everly's heart thudded. *Totally fine. Just realizing that I'm head over heels in love with you, and
it's terrifying. Also, surprise! We're having twins.*

"I'm great, but I think I'm ready for that walk
now." She needed to put some distance between her-

self and so many glittering engagement rings. She definitely shouldn't have let Henry slide one onto her finger. She was beginning to get crazy ideas in her head.

The thing was, those ideas didn't *feel* so crazy. They felt nice. Perfect, actually. If Everly didn't know better, she almost might have believed they were destined to come true. Like marrying Henry might have been part of fate's grand plan all along and they'd been barreling toward this moment from the very second they'd first met. Like Henry just might be her soulmate.

"I think I need to get some air," she blurted.

"Okay." Henry nodded, worry creasing his brow. "I'll try and find you a glass of ice water. Meet you out front in just a minute?"

"Thank you." Everly nodded and rushed toward the entrance to the store, clutching the little blue box to her chest.

Everything around her seemed too bright all of a sudden, too sparkly. She needed to remove herself from the dreamy, magic spell she'd fallen under and get back to real life, where she and Henry were on even ground and there was no risk whatsoever of having her heart broken.

Deep breaths. Just a few more steps.

The doorman bid her goodbye, and she all but stumbled out onto the busy sidewalk, where real life was ready and waiting for her...

In the form of the man she'd almost married.

* * *

"Gregory." Everly nearly stumbled directly into him but caught herself just in time.

What was her ex-fiancé doing here? Shouldn't he be at his yacht club? Or perhaps running out on a wedding somewhere and leaving another woman's life in tatters?

"Everly," Gregory said with an unmistakable hint of pity in his voice.

Irritation seared through her. The last thing she wanted was for Gregory to feel sorry for her. She didn't need or want his pity.

"So nice to run into you," she said evenly.

He shifted from one foot to the other, gaze flitting from the blue box in her hands to the elegant lettering across the marquis that spelled out Tiffany & Co. "Tiffany's, huh? You always did love that old movie starring Katharine Hepburn."

"*Audrey* Hepburn," she corrected. *Which you would know if you'd ever watched the film with me.* Honestly, what had she ever seen in this man?

"Right, right." He nodded.

Behind Everly, the doorman swished opened the glass double doors again and a rush of cool air hit the back of her neck. Gregory's attention seemed to snag on something over her shoulder.

"Is that—" His eyes went flinty. "Of course it is. I should've known."

"What?" Everly's annoyance flared. She didn't

want to be having this conversation. In a city of millions, why did she have to run into Gregory, of all people? Today, of all days?

He was a nuisance, more than anything. As she stood opposite Gregory, she almost felt like she didn't know him anymore. He was like a stranger— a stranger who no longer had the power to break her heart. He never really had, not like Henry did.

"I was just passing by on my way to a meeting and spotted you as you were coming out of Tiffany's. You're here with Aston," Gregory said, eyes narrowing on a spot in the distance, back inside the jewelry store.

For reasons Everly had never clearly understood, Gregory always called Henry by his last name instead of his first. She'd always assumed it was simply a guy thing. But seeing his pinched expression as he peered into the store almost made her feel like he was jealous.

Gregory crossed his arms, eyes narrowing as his gaze zeroed in on the necklace with the E charm hanging around her neck. "So are you two together now?"

Everly squared her shoulders. "That's none of your business. Nothing I do is any of your concern whatsoever anymore. You walked out in the middle of our wedding, remember?"

His brows knitted. "Don't you want to know why?"

Not particularly. The wedding seemed like ancient

history at this point. Everly had enough to worry about on this very day without dredging up their nonmarriage. "We don't have to do this, Gregory. Truly. I'm sure you had your reasons."

"Reason, singular," Gregory nodded toward the glossy store windows. "Him."

"Henry?" Everly didn't understand. Gregory knew how long she and Henry had been friends. She'd explained to him back when they first starting dating that she and Henry didn't have any romantic history at all. They were friends, plain and simple.

Of course things had gotten progressively more complicated since her wedding night.

"Yes, Everly. Are you really that surprised?" Gregory's tone softened a bit as he gave her an expectant look.

Yes, she started to say, but something held her back.

"I should have seen it sooner. I wish I had—it probably would have saved both of us a lot of grief. I didn't mean to hurt you, Everly. I really didn't. Something felt off in the lead-up to the wedding, and I couldn't put my finger on what it was. Then we were standing there in the ballroom of the Plaza, and you started walking down the aisle and I realized you were looking at him instead of me."

Everly couldn't have been more shocked if he'd slapped her right across the face. "No."

"Yes." Gregory nodded. "Your eyes darted to me

soon enough, but the first person your gaze landed on was Henry. I saw it as clear as day."

"I—" Everly didn't know what to say. "He was my man of honor."

Her man of honor, as if that covered it. But maybe it did. The honor part, at least. Henry had always been her knight in shining armor. Maybe that hadn't left as much room for a man in her life as she'd thought it had.

"I tried to overlook it. I really did, because I believed you when you told me that you and Henry were just close friends. Was I crazy about the fact that you wanted him to be your man of honor so badly that we had to schedule our wedding around Henry's travel calendar? Not particularly. It seemed to me that Addison would've made a fine maid of honor. She's your sister, after all. And you two are certainly close." He ran a hand through his hair and dodged a man with a briefcase who was barreling down the sidewalk. "But I dealt with it because it was important to you. *He* was important to you. I just didn't realize quite how much until the wedding."

She took a deep breath and pressed the blue box to her heart in an effort to try and slow down her pulse. Her heart was galloping like a herd of wild horses. It couldn't be good for the baby.

Babies, remember? Plural.

So this was why Gregory had stopped sleeping with her in the months leading up to the wedding.

His behavior suddenly seemed crystal clear. Her fiancé had been jealous of Henry all along. Their wedding day had simply been the icing on the cake.

"Anyway, it was Henry's expression that was the dead giveaway. I watched him watching you as you walked down the aisle, and there was no mistaking it. In that moment, everything became as clear as day. He's in love with you," Gregory said.

Everly went completely still. The crush of pedestrians trying to maneuver their way around them went blurry. This was all a lot to digest. Too much, if she was really being honest. She'd had the shock of her life this morning at the obstetrician's office, and just a few minutes ago, her true feelings for Henry had hit her like a ton of bricks. Her emotional bandwidth was razor thin.

"But you already know that by now, don't you?" Gregory's eyebrows crept closer to his hairline.

Everly swallowed.

She didn't want to talk about Henry with Gregory. She wasn't sure herself what was going on between them. How could she possibly explain it to someone else? Especially the man who'd ditched her at the altar.

"Gregory, we could have talked all of this out on our wedding day, but you chose to leave instead," she said as calmly as she could manage.

That was the truth, and it always would be. He could blame her all he wanted, but she hadn't been the one to walk out and leave him all alone in front of their family and friends.

"You're right. I could've handled things better. I'm sorry for that." Gregory nodded, and then his eyes turned sympathetic again. The pity she'd seen earlier in his expression was on full display now. "But I hope you know what you're getting yourself into with him. You'll never be able to rely on Henry, not really. You do realize that, don't you?"

She reeled back on her pretty snow globe heels and nearly collided with a group of tourists busy taking photos of the Fifth Avenue street sign.

"I know you think he's always there for you, but ask yourself: Is he really? The guy can't even put down roots for longer than five minutes. What's going to happen when you need him—*really* need him—and he's off in Croatia or the Canary Islands or Sri Lanka?"

Or Antarctica.

A cold chill washed over Everly. She bit down hard on the inside of her cheek to keep her teeth from chattering.

"I know you think I'm the bad guy here." Gregory let out a ragged breath. "And maybe I am. But you need to take a good long look at your boyfriend and ask yourself if he's the future you really want. Believe it or not, I only want what's best for you. I do care about you, Everly."

His voice broke when he said her name, and Everly

had to wrap her arms around herself and look away. Gregory had just given voice to her worst fears— the thoughts she struggled to ignore when she woke up at night and berated herself for not telling Henry about the pregnancy yet.

Those thoughts and fears sounded far worse coming out of Gregory's mouth. Everly's first instinct was to tell him he was wrong. Henry was a good man, the very best she'd ever known. He wasn't the selfish wanderer that Gregory made him out to be. She could count on him. She always could.

But Dr. Calderon had made things very clear earlier—all multiple pregnancies were considered high risk. There were a host of things that could wrong, both for the mother and for the babies. If Everly was faced with a sudden medical crisis, could Henry get back from wherever his newest adventure took him in time to be with her?

Rogue attack penguins were suddenly the least of her problems.

"I know you think Henry's lifestyle is noble and that he chose to do what he does as a way to honor his dead father. But before you run off and marry him or, heaven forbid, have children with him, remember this…" Gregory's voice dropped to a near whisper. "He's no Prince Charming and he's certainly no family man."

Everly blinked. She wasn't even sure she'd heard him correctly, but before she could react, Henry was suddenly at her side holding a cup of ice water and glaring at Gregory like he wanted to throttle him.

"Hello, Gregory," he said, through gritted teeth.

Had Henry heard what Gregory had just said? Everly didn't think so. If he had, she felt like he'd have some choice words in response. But the fact that Gregory was there at all, speaking to her, obviously didn't sit well with him.

"Aston." Gregory's attempt at a smile was more of a grimace. He gave Henry a curt nod.

Henry ignored the gesture and turned toward Everly, handing her the water. "E, are you okay?"

No. Not remotely okay.

"Is this guy bothering you, because—" Henry started, but Everly held up a hand to cut him off.

"It's fine. Honestly. Gregory was just leaving." Her lips curved into a tight smile as she let herself look at her former fiancé for what she hoped was the last time in her entire life. "Weren't you, Gregory?"

"If that's what you want, then yes," Gregory said as he gave them both a slow nod. "Goodbye, Everly."

Then he flashed her another of those pitying smiles that made her want to scream into a pillow— except Everly didn't feel like screaming this time. She felt more like crying, and worse, she wasn't altogether sure why.

Chapter Fourteen

Henry didn't like the lost look on Everly's face as Gregory Hoyt walked away. Nor did Henry like the fact that he hadn't been right there, by her side, when she'd evidently run into her ex on the sidewalk. One look at their exchange had been all it took to know that whatever that jerk had been saying to her had upset Everly in a major way.

He cupped her elbow, and she blinked as if she'd fallen into a trance.

"E, seriously. Talk to me." Henry's gut was still fully clenched, but somewhere beyond the adrenaline surging through his body from going into full protective mode, he was vaguely aware of an ice-cold trickle of dread snaking its way up his spine. "What just happened?"

Everly took an excruciatingly slow sip of her water. The Tiffany's box containing the silver charm for Holly was still curled against her chest. Henry lived and died a thousand deaths as he waited for her to say something.

Whatever had transpired between her and Gregory while he'd been inside the store hadn't been good. That much was clear. Everly's face was as white as a sheet.

"It was nothing." She shook her head. "I came outside, and we just sort of ran into each other. Just a freak coincidence."

"I hope he was kind to you," Henry said, although he wasn't holding his breath.

The guy had walked out on her mid-ceremony, and from what Henry knew, Everly hadn't spoken to him since. In the seven weeks since the wedding, Gregory hadn't reached out to make sure she was okay, nor had he apologized for his actions. Expecting him to be thoughtful or considerate of Everly's feelings at this point seemed like a stretch.

"I'm sure he thought he was being kind," Everly said, and her face flushed with color.

He knew it. Henry had been certain Gregory had rattled her, whether intentionally or not. He was betting on intentionally. Whatever goodwill Henry had felt for Gregory had withered and died the moment he'd set eyes on Everly's tearstained face when she answered his knock at the door of the honeymoon suite on her wedding night.

"Let's go home, darling." He wrapped an arm around her shoulders, but instead of melting into him, she went the slightest bit rigid.

Everly's forehead puckered. "Home? What about our walk?"

"You don't seem all that up for it, and that's fine. I don't mind hanging out at home, ordering in food and putting one of your comfort watches on the television." He blew her a little kiss. "Again."

He was angling for a laugh or, at the very least, a smile. Neither was forthcoming.

"I still really need to talk to you," she said, and for the first time, Henry began to wonder if whatever she needed to tell him might be bad news. "Let's go to the park like we planned, okay?"

"Sure." Henry released his hold on her shoulders and tucked his hands into his trouser pockets. Something about this didn't feel right—not at all. "I'm up for anything."

They walked a few blocks without speaking, side by side. With each step, Henry itched to take Everly's hand in his. If he could just touch her, just weave her fingers through his, maybe he could anchor her to the here and now…keep her with him for a little bit longer. But with the blue box in one hand and the cup of water in the other, he couldn't. Every so often as they walked, his fingertips brushed against the frothy tulle of her dress, causing a tingle to run up every square inch of his arm.

Everly seemed as far away as ever. Henry tried several times to catch her gaze with his, but she never seemed to glance his way. She was laser focused on moving forward, glittery shoes eating up the pavement. And suddenly, as if it had sprung right up out of nowhere, the sparkling entrance to the Plaza Hotel lay right in front of them.

Henry had been so preoccupied wondering what was going on in Everly's head that he'd forgotten their path to the park would take them right past the grand hotel. Everly had, too, apparently, as both of their footsteps slowed to a stop just opposite the valet area.

Time stood still as Henry stared at the crimson carpeted steps, the gleaming Art Deco–style doors and grand columns flanking the entrance. A knot lodged in this throat, and if he could've had one wish, it would have been for the hands on the Cartier watch his dad had given him to spin backwards, tick-tock-tick, to seven weeks prior—to the morning he'd kissed Everly goodbye at that very spot and put her in one of the yellow taxi cabs that sat ready and waiting to whisk guests away from the opulent building…away from the honeymoon suite…away from what could have been.

His eyes narrowed and his heart pounded as his gaze bore into the dazzling hotel. Maybe if he stared hard enough, he could summon the ghosts of their former selves, exiting the building hand in hand, dressed in their wedding clothes from the night before. Henry could take himself by the shoulders and give the man in the crumpled tuxedo a hard shake.

What are you doing, man? Don't leave. Don't get on that plane. Stay here and make things right. Can't you see that she's scared?

That's what he would have said, given the chance. And then Henry would have climbed into the cab beside Everly and kissed her hard enough to steam up the windows as they rode off into the sunrise together.

Time didn't work that way, though. There was no going back, and now all he could do was glance at Everly, search out her gaze and try and see if she, too, wished things had gone differently that morning.

Slowly, her gaze flitted toward his, and the unshed tears he saw welling up in her eyes nearly killed him.

"E, that morning," he said, clutching his heart. "If I could do it all over again, I—"

"Please don't." Everly shook her head, and a single tear spilled over, leaving a torturous trail down her porcelain cheek. "Don't say it."

It was the same thing she'd said last time, the very morning in question—the morning after they'd first made love. That's what it had been for Henry. Not just comfort, not just sex. Love, from the very bottom of his heart.

He'd done as she asked and kept silent last time, but he couldn't anymore. She needed to hear what he had to say. He needed to get it off his chest, and she needed to know about the regret he'd been carrying around for the past seven weeks.

"If I could do it all over again, I wouldn't have left for Bora-Bora," he said bluntly.

Everly's eyelashes fluttered, but her attempt to keep herself from crying failed miserably. A second teardrop fell, and then another. Each one felt like a blow to Henry's chest.

"But you did leave," she said through her tears.

He raked a hand through his hair, tugging hard at the ends. "Yeah, I did. And I'm sorry. I've regretted it ever since. You told me to pretend the night before had never happened. You told me to go."

Everly shook her head. "I never said that."

Henry scrubbed his face. Was she joking? He'd replayed every word they'd uttered to each other over and over in his head for weeks. "You did, darling. You said, and I quote, 'Let's just pretend last night never happened, okay? And let's definitely not talk about it. Ever.'"

He could still see her in that plush hotel bathrobe, so oversized on her that its hem trailed behind her like the train on a wedding gown. She'd been tousled and gorgeous, and it had taken every ounce of self-control Henry possessed not to kiss her fears away and slide his hands inside that thick terrycloth, just to feel the warmth of her again. Warm…wonder-ful…*his*.

"Oh, I know I said that part. I mean I never told you to leave and go to Bora-Bora. You asked me to go with you, and I told you I couldn't." Everly made a sad attempt at a smile. The way her chin quivered was nearly the death of him. "But I never told you to go."

Henry's entire body went leaden.

Was that true?

It must be. Everly seemed entirely certain.

"It's okay, though. I'm telling you now," Everly said.

"I'm not following," Henry said, even as his heart started knocking around so hard in his chest that he thought it might pound right out of him.

"I'm telling you to go." Everly took a ragged inhale and averted her gaze away from the hotel. "I didn't want to do this here, but what I have to say can't wait any longer, Henry. I've waited far too long, and you're going to be angry with me, and that's perfectly understandable. But I can't keep pretending this is a date or a cozy walk to the park. I have to just go ahead and do it now."

Henry knew better than to interrupt, which was fine, because he'd never been at such a loss for words in his life. He still didn't have a clue what was going on, but he knew without a doubt that he wasn't going to like it.

"Henry, I'm pregnant. We're having twins." For the briefest moment, there was a glimmer of joy in Everly's gaze, and even though Henry was reeling at the news, in that sublime second, he'd never been happier. *Pregnant...twins.* He was going to be a dad. He and Everly were going to be a family—a real one, at long last.

Then she tore her gaze from his, and Henry realized everything wasn't going to turn out the way he'd hoped...the way it was meant to be.

"I think it would be best if you take the assignment in Antarctica," Everly said. "I think the distance and time apart is just what we need. This time, I really am telling you to go."

Everly's entire body trembled from the effort it had taken to get the words out. As it turned out, telling Henry about the pregnancy wasn't the hardest thing she'd ever had to say to him. Telling him to leave was far, far more difficult.

"I don't understand," Henry said, eyes blazing.

"I know. I should've told you right away. I just found out the night before you showed up at the *Veil* offices, and then I fainted, and everything got so complicated. I kept trying, and every time I tried to get the words out, something would happen and I just couldn't. Then last night..." A sob wracked her body, but she took a shuddering breath and kept going. "...was wonderful. Last night was perfect, but it shouldn't have ever happened—not until after I'd told you I was pregnant. Then this morning, I had my first prenatal appointment and found out I'm carrying twins, and that's it. Now you know everything."

Henry shook his head. His posture was suddenly stiffer and more rigid than Everly had ever seen it before. "No, not everything. Not even close. You just fully skipped over the part where you told me to move to Antarctica for six months."

She nodded. Maybe if she nodded hard enough, she'd be able to convince herself she was doing the right thing. "You should go. We need time and space to figure this out. We're going to be co-parents to twin infants, and you live in a completely different country. It's going to be challenging, and I just think the longer that we play house, the harder it will be when everything goes back to normal."

"Is that what we've been doing?" Henry arched an eyebrow. The set of his jaw was suddenly as hard as granite. "Playing house?"

Everly's legs felt like they might collapse beneath her. She walked past him and sat down on a nearby bench, which unfortunately provided her with a full-on view of the Plaza Hotel, the place where all of this had started.

Who do you think you're kidding? This started way before your wedding night. It started years ago.

Everly squeezed her eyes shut. She didn't want to think about all the years that stretched between them—all the feelings, all the memories. If she did, she'd never be able to see this through.

It would have been so much easier to push him away if he'd been someone else. *Anyone* else.

She opened her eyes and forced herself to look at him, now standing directly in front of the bench with his back to the hotel so he could see her face. Or maybe he simply wanted to put the Plaza and everything it meant firmly behind him. She wouldn't blame him if he did.

"Yes, that's what we've been doing. When you're living together for a limited amount of time and you both know there's no real future together, it's called playing house," she said.

"Who said we don't have a future together?" A vein throbbed to life in Henry's left temple. "Of course we do. You're my—"

He abruptly stopped speaking, as if he weren't sure how to complete the thought.

"I'm your what?" Everly asked, certain she didn't really want to know. Either way, the answer would be a heartbreaker.

Henry collapsed onto the bench beside her and dropped his head into his hands. She could feel the angst coming off him in waves. The effort it took not to wrap her arms around him and beg him to forget the things she was saying was almost too much to bear.

"Do you really want me to say it, E? For the first

time, right here, right now…when you're breaking my heart?" When he lifted his head and turned to look at her, his eyes were rimmed bright red. The sight of Henry like that was an arrow straight to Everly's heart. In all the time she'd known him, Everly had never seen Henry cry. Not once. "Because I will. You're my best friend. You're going to be the mother of my children. And you're the love of my life. That's who you are to me, sweetheart. I'm in love with you."

She shook her head. *No.* She didn't want to hear this. She couldn't take it. As long as they kept pretending there was nothing but friendship between them, she could come out of this unscathed. But Henry had just gone and ruined everything by laying himself bare and putting their entire relationship on the line.

You're breaking my heart…

Out of all the things he'd just said, that one resonated most of all. Those were the words that Everly would never forget for the rest of her life. Not the nice things, not the lovely things, but the fact that she'd broken the only man she'd ever truly loved.

"Henry, you don't mean that. It's the pregnancy. It's a lot to take in, and you might think you love me right now, but—"

"Don't," he said as his eyes went even redder. "Don't tell me how I feel. Believe me, I'm well aware of the feelings I have for you, E. I've been holding them in for quite some time."

Everly bit her tongue and looked away. Big mistake—now the hotel was directly in her line of vision. Her gaze flitted automatically to the top floor, where the honeymoon suite was located. Memories of the night they'd spent there together pressed in, threatening to undo all the damage she'd just done.

It wasn't too late, was it? She could tell Henry she didn't mean any of it. She could crawl into his lap and kiss away the pain etched in his handsome features and they could start over, do it right this time.

And then what?

They'd be right back to where they started, leaving Everly more vulnerable and—ultimately—alone, at a time in her life when she needed to be strong. Stronger than she'd ever been before.

"Henry, I don't want you to quit traveling. I can't ask you to do that," she said quietly.

"What about what I want?" His eyes bore into her so hard that she was sure he could see inside her head and tell that was she was lying through her teeth. Lying about everything.

Of course she didn't want him to go to Antarctica. But Gregory's words of warning had stoked every insecurity and fear she'd been trying her best not to think about. Seeing him again had been a potent reminder of what happened when you trusted someone with your heart only to have them stomp all over it.

She'd lost every man she'd ever cared about, every

man she'd ever trusted—either by choice or by fate. Every man, except one.

Everly wasn't going to let it happen again. This time, she'd be the one to decide when her heart broke. At least it wouldn't come as such a surprise this time around. Better for things to end now, before they really started, than to wait until she forgot what her bed felt like without Henry Aston in it.

"E, say something," Henry said. "Please. I know this isn't what you want. Let me be there for you and the babies. As a friend, as a lover—however you'll have me. Just don't try and push me away."

If only it were that simple. If only Everly could call her best friend Henry and tell him about the gigantic mistake she was making and beg him to help her figure out how to turn things back around, how to let herself be loved.

But Henry wasn't that friend anymore. Everly had tried so hard to not let him become anything more that she'd ended up losing him altogether. Friends didn't break each other's hearts. Friends told the truth. Friends didn't keep secrets.

"We'll figure out a plan for the babies when you get back from Antarctica. By then, we'll both be over—" she waved a hand back and forth between them "—whatever this is."

Another lie. She'd never be over Henry.

Hurt glittered in Henry's eyes, bluer than blue. "And until then? What happens between now and the trip? We're just supposed to live together and work together, all the while knowing that we're having children together but keep pretending we're not in love?"

"I think it's probably best that you check into a hotel for the rest of the time you're in New York." Everly turned to take one last look at him so she could memorize the angles of his face, the cut of his jaw and the exact curve of his bottom lip, as if she hadn't already tucked those details into her heart and locked them away a long, long time ago. "And I never said I was in love with you."

Henry smiled, and it was the saddest, most devastating thing Everly had ever seen. "You didn't have to."

Chapter Fifteen

Three weeks later, Henry sat at the desk in his suite at the Plaza and thumbed through the brochure for the Antarctica trip. The photographs were stunning, promising a world of jagged peaks, cool blue glaciers and a sheet of ice so thick and so white that it looked like a polar desert. His father wouldn't have believed his eyes. In all his travels, Henry had never seen anything quite like it.

He'd also never been less enthusiastic about a trip in his entire career.

He flipped the brochure closed, pushed it aside and skimmed through his email on his laptop. His inbox was virtually empty. The honeymoon pull-out feature for *Veil*'s June issue was completely fin-ished—two weeks ahead of schedule.

Henry had only shown his face in the *Veil* office once since his breakup with Everly. That's what he was calling it in his head—a breakup, even though they'd never officially been a couple. What else was he supposed to call it when he'd felt like his heart had literally broken up into shards, scattered all over the sidewalk in front of the Plaza?

Right after Everly reminded him that she'd never told him she loved him, Henry had gotten up, walked straight into the hotel lobby and checked into a suite. Not the honeymoon suite, obviously. He wasn't that much of a glutton for punishment. He hadn't been thinking clearly at the time, though. He'd just found out he was going to be a father and lost the love of his life, all in one fell swoop. He hadn't so much walked up to the reception desk as staggered toward it like a member of the walking wounded. When he'd woken up the next morning, he'd vowed to change hotels the minute he got off work.

Henry hadn't changed hotels, though. He was still there, at the Plaza, working remotely from his suite because he wanted to give Everly the space she seemed to think she needed. At least that's what he told himself, because it was easier to believe he was acting nobly than admit to himself that he simply couldn't bear to see her. The morning after the breakup, he'd shown up to the office bright and early, certain that Everly would seek him out and admit that she loved him. He understood she was frightened.

Having twins was a huge life-altering event, and the way they'd started their family hadn't exactly been the easiest or most traditional beginning. He knew she needed time.

But the way she'd looked right through him when they'd passed in the hallway had done him in. He'd gone straight to his office, shot off an email to Colette to inform her that he'd be working remotely from that point forward, and then he'd packed up his briefcase and left.

Since then—other than a few ill-advised evenings spent at the hotel bar—Henry had scarcely left the building. There'd been a few working lunches with Colette, which had always taken place at a restaurant instead of the office. Otherwise, he stayed put. Irony of ironies, after being dumped for his wandering ways, Henry had become the world's most boring homebody, seemingly overnight.

Deep down, he knew his travel schedule wasn't the whole problem. There was a whole host of things going on in Everly's head, and Henry couldn't help but think that whatever Gregory had said to her outside of Tiffany's had contributed to her decision to try and keep him at arm's length. But how could Henry fix things when she wouldn't tell him what was wrong?

Don't you know her well enough to realize why she thinks she needs to handle things all on her own?

Henry did know—at least he thought he did. It all

went back to the conversation they'd had over *cacio e pepe* when he'd first come back to New York. She'd told him she was tired of feeling like she wasn't lovable enough for anyone to stick around, and Henry had thought she'd been talking about losing her dad. Gregory abandoning her during the wedding had reopened old wounds that had taken years to heal. Henry understood those sort of wounds better than most people did.

What he hadn't understood was that she'd also been talking about him. Maybe not consciously, but somewhere beneath the surface, she'd wanted him to stay the morning after the wedding instead of jumping on a plane like he always did. What killed Henry was that getting on that plane had been the last thing he'd wanted to do.

But he'd done it anyway.

Maybe that's why he couldn't bring himself to leave the Plaza now that he'd moved in. Perhaps he thought that staying here was somehow undoing the fact that he'd walked out of those gilded doors mere hours after making love to Everly without putting up a fight. Maybe he just missed her. Maybe he wanted to stay here because it was the only place he felt close to her anymore.

Or maybe it was all of those things, and Henry was just a tragic mess.

He swallowed hard and fired off one last email to Colette, thanking her for the opportunity to work on the June issue, acknowledging the nice things she'd said about the finalized version of the honeymoon feature and covering one other important matter of business. He'd delivered his final work product the night before, just past 11:00 p.m., and by 8:00 a.m., she'd already gone over the entire seventy-five pages of editorial and loved every word of it. Colette was a beast. He wondered when she slept. Then again, he hadn't gotten much sleep in recent weeks himself.

Colette had also been thrilled that he'd pulled off the project under budget and well ahead of deadline. Working kept Henry occupied. It kept him from thinking. He wished he could figure out a way to keep himself from feeling, too.

Sooner or later, he'd have to see Everly again. He couldn't leave the country without saying goodbye, and they still needed to talk about her pregnancy. He'd been holding out hope that she might come to him and, at the very least, try and rekindle their friendship.

But time was running out. He'd already pushed his luck with his editor at *Wanderlust* as far as he possibly could. If Henry didn't give him an answer about Antarctica today, he might end up living at the Plaza the rest of his natural life because he wouldn't have a job in London to go back to.

He picked up his cell and scrolled until he got to the contact information for his editor, Paul Wood.

Paul answered on the first ring. "Henry, it's about

damn time. I was beginning to wonder if we'd lost you to *Veil* for good."

"We've actually already wrapped up the travel section of the issue," Henry said, gaze still trained on the laptop screen and his inbox.

"Excellent. So you're free earlier than expected. That's fantastic news. There's a ship headed to the Drake Passage in just a few days. This could be it—the story that finally wins you a Wolf Granger Award," Paul said, appealing to Henry's sense of ambition. Five nominations, five losses. Henry had always imagined standing on that esteemed stage and giving an acceptance speech in which he talked about his father and thanked him for instilling him with a love of adventure and a sense of purpose. Alas, Henry still hadn't gotten that opportunity. "Please tell me you've got an answer for me, Henry."

Henry's email pinged with an incoming message—the one he'd been waiting for. He skimmed it, and then his gaze drifted toward the brochure. *Welcome to Antarctica!* Continent number six of seven. "As a matter of fact, I do."

Fashion closet. 15 minutes.

The text pinged on Everly's phone just as she and Holly drew near to the private dog park around the corner from their apartment.

Everly's discovery of the dog park just two days after the painful discussion with Henry in front of the Plaza had been a godsend. For the first forty-eight hours after sending Henry away, she'd walked through life in a fog. The day after their breakup, when Everly had passed Henry in the hallway at the office, she'd been so rattled that she couldn't even look him in the eye. It was just too painful, so she'd fixed her gaze on an invisible spot on the horizon and plowed ahead as if they were strangers.

It hadn't been her finest moment. She'd cried her eyes out for two solid hours in the fashion closet directly afterward.

In the weeks since, Everly had barely been able to function. Colette had made her rewrite her article about the Tiffany & Co. event three times. Both her job and her sanity were now hanging by a thread, and for all practical purposes, the only things holding her together were the *Veil* girls, her dog and the knowledge that she needed to stay healthy for her babies.

Henry's babies, she reminded herself on a near constant basis—as if she could forget. Then she'd imagine children with Henry's blue eyes, his kind and generous heart, and his love for adventure, and she'd turn into a crying mess all over again.

Holly's tail wagged, and she tugged at the end of her leash as they approached the wrought iron gate of the small dog area of the park. At six in the morning, the park was deserted, but Holly didn't seem to care. She loved zipping around the grassy space, chasing squirrels as they scrambled along the branches of the cherry blossom trees swaying overhead. The half hour that Everly and Holly spent here every morning before work was the best part of Everly's day. Sometimes Everly even caught herself smiling.

Not now, though.

The early morning 911 text had caught her off guard. Didn't Addison know what time it was? What could have possibly happened to warrant an emergency summons to the office before the coffee truck even opened for business?

Everly clicked the gate shut behind her, unclipped Holly's leash and perched on the edge of one of the dog park's Victorian-style benches to tap out a reply.

Do you realize it's 6 in the morning?

Three little dots appeared in the group text chat, indicating that either Addison or Daphne was typing a response. Everly's money was on Addison, workaholic to her very core.

Sure enough, a text pinged from Addison less than a second later.

Yes, I do. Get here ASAP. We all know you're not sleeping anyway.

Harsh but accurate.

I'm at the dog park with Holly. My hair is in a messy bun and I'm wearing sweatpants.

They were cute Kate Spade sweats decorated with little embroidered lemons, but still. If she turned up at the *Veil* office in this getup, Colette would think she'd had a complete and total breakdown.

Which wasn't altogether inaccurate.

Come anyway. Bring Holly. You know the rules, Addison texted back.

Everly sighed. She did, indeed, know the rules. A fashion closet emergency text was serious—like the Bat Signal, only with tulle, organza and sequins instead of Lycra superhero unitards. Addison and Daphne had always shown up for Everly when she'd activated such a critical call for help. She owed it to them to show up.

"Holly Golightly," she called in a singsong voice, and the little Cavalier bounded toward her, ears flying. "Let's go, girl. Today's the day you officially become a member of the *Veil* crew."

By some miracle, they arrived within the fifteen-minute time mandate. Everly's bun had progressed from messy to total disaster, and Holly's long silky ears were littered with pink cherry blossom petals, but they'd made it. Despite the early hour, Addison was fully in Colette 2.0 mode, immaculately dressed in a slim pinstriped pencil skirt and sky-high Chanel pumps with bold pearl detailing on the heels. Daphne's look landed somewhere in between. Her vintage-inspired A-line dress had a colorful dinosaur print. The cotton-candy highlights in her hair really brought out the pink velociraptors mingled in and among yellow T-rexes and tangerine stegosauruses.

"Wow, when you said you looked like a mess, you weren't kidding, were you?" Addison reached to pluck a twig from what was left of Everly's bun.

"Gee, thanks. You remember that I'm pregnant, right? With twins?" Everly rested her hand on her growing belly. "Ultrastretch fabric is my friend these days."

Daphne grinned at her. "You look amazing, Everly."

"She looks exhausted," Addison corrected.

"Is that why we're here?" Everly glanced back and forth between them. "To critique my appearance?"

"No, sweetie." Daphne smiled again, but there was a hint of concern in her eyes that made Everly go on high alert.

"Wait a minute. *Is* this about me?" Everly dropped onto the brocade ottoman, and Holly flung herself immediately onto her lap. "I thought maybe we were here to discuss Daphne's ongoing battle with the fact checker."

"Ew, no." Daphne rolled her eyes. "Although, he's been more annoying than ever lately. Would you believe that yesterday he actually tried to convince me that the first red lipstick was actually made out of beetles? Disgusting."

"Wait." Addison tilted her head. "Isn't that factoid technically accurate?"

"Yes, but that's beside the point. He's still annoying," Daphne said, and her cheeks flushed as a pink as the velociraptors romping all over the fitted bodice of her dress.

Everly bit back a smile. She had a feeling they hadn't heard the last of Daphne's know-it-all office nemesis.

"Actually, yes. This meeting is about you." Addison winced. "And Henry."

A pang coursed through Everly at the sound of his name. She gathered Holly in her arms and stood. "Nope. Not today, you guys. I can't. We've talked about this already, and you both know how I feel."

Everly had of course filled them both in on everything that had transpired between her and Henry. In the age-old tradition of breakups everywhere, they'd shared cartons of ice cream and gone through numerous boxes of Kleenex that Daphne had borrowed from *Veil*'s beauty department. Everly knew that Addison and Daphne both thought she'd done the wrong thing, but like true friends, they'd promised to respect her decision. *You just need some time to adjust to all the changes happening in your life right now,* they'd said. *You'll realize soon enough that you and Henry belong together.*

Maybe she would, but Everly doubted it. As excruciating as it had been, she'd done the right thing. Everly still wanted Henry. She wanted him so bad she couldn't see straight. Every day was a struggle to resist the urge to hunt him down and beg him to come home. She *loved* Henry. She just loved him too much to try and change him. He wanted travel and adventure and (metaphorical) penguins, and she wanted a home. She wanted a nursery with matching cribs, mint-colored gingham wallpaper and a rocking chair by the window overlooking the dog park. She wanted to stay and make a name for herself at *Veil*, assuming she didn't get fired first. Most of all, she wanted her best friend Henry back.

Everly didn't see how that was possible. Those days were over. But she couldn't let go of her feelings for him, and she knew she never would. Henry was the father of her children, and he was her soulmate, even if she'd never be able to bring herself to tell him that.

Instead, she'd taken the H charm that he'd bought for Holly and slid the delicate silver initial onto the chain that held her E charm. E and H, for Everly and Henry, forever side by side, pressed close to her heart. Her little secret.

"Everly, we're not trying to pressure you one way or another. But there's something you need to see," Daphne said, and then her gaze slid toward Addison.

Addison took a deep breath, bent over her massive Louis Vuitton handbag—situated on the brocade ottoman in all of its LV monogrammed glory—and plucked a sheaf of papers from its confines. "Here."

She thrust the papers toward Everly.

Everly didn't make a move to take them. Her

stomach churned just thinking about what the type-written pages could possibly contain. "You're going to have to give me a little more information before I read whatever that is."

"It's the interview Colette did with Henry for the June issue. This is the final edited version. It's already been typeset and sent off to the printers. You need to see it, Everly, and it really can't wait until the magazine hits the stands," Addison said.

Everly's breath shook. Her fingers closed around the stack of papers before she could stop herself. "I'm not supposed to see this, though. This is proprietary information. Only senior editorial staff are allowed to review final, unpublished pages before the issue goes to print."

Everly wasn't telling Addison anything she didn't already know, but she couldn't fathom why her sister—a beacon of journalistic integrity and girl boss icon in the making—would violate company policy like this.

"Correct," Addison said with a nod.

"You could get fired for showing it to me," Everly said bluntly.

"I know, and it would be worth it." Addison reached to tuck a stray chunk of Everly's hair back into her bun. "You're my baby sister, and you need to know the truth about Henry before it's too late. If it costs me my job, then so be it."

Everly shook her head as a weight settled on her

heart. She was walking on the thinnest possible ice at *Veil*. The last thing she wanted was to do something that might jeopardize her sister's career. Addison's job meant everything to her. "I don't know what to say."

"Don't say anything." Addison gathered her handbag and slung it over her shoulder. She and Daphne moved toward the door, clearly intent on letting Everly absorb Henry's interview in private. "Just read."

And so she did.

Chapter Sixteen

Everly wasn't sure how long she sat in the fashion closet going over Henry's interview with a fine-toothed comb. At first, she'd skimmed its contents, more than familiar with Henry's background, which Colette had placed heavy emphasis on in the opening paragraphs. She wrote about his college days at Columbia and his time spent on the school paper. Benign stuff that wouldn't come as a surprise to anyone remotely familiar with Henry's bio in *Wanderlust*.

But by the third paragraph, Everly already found herself reading with her heart in her throat. Henry had shared the story of his father's illness with Colette. It was right there in black and white for all the world to see. He'd even shown Colette the inscription on the back of his Cartier, and she'd included the transcript of the full poem where the Tolkien quote had been lifted.

The snippet was from *The Lord of the Rings*, and the poem was called "All That Glitters Is Not Gold." Henry had said he liked to remind himself of the meaning of the full poem, not just the part about wandering that had meant so much to his father. The message was a warning, Henry had said. It meant that not everything was as it appeared. Sometimes people went their entire lives without realizing they held something precious in their hands because they were too busy being preoccupied by the bright and shiny distractions around them.

The papers shook in Everly's hands as she continued reading.

"I don't want to reach the end of my life and realize I missed the treasure that was right there, all along," Aston says, and his eyes go dark—dark enough for me to know there's a story there. A story that hasn't reached its full denouement.

"What's your treasure?" I ask him. "You've traveled all over the globe. You've seen more of the world than most people see in a lifetime. What glitters most of all for Henry Aston?"

He answers without hesitation. "Not a place but a woman—a friend. My best friend, actually, but someone I've just recently realized I'm in love with."

"I hope she has your same spirit of adventure," I tell him.

Henry laughs and shakes his head. "Adventure means different things to different people. I'm thankful to my father for teaching me to appreciate different cultures and to experience many ways of life and see the wonders of this earth that not many people get to experience. But after a lifetime of wandering the globe, I've come to realize that life's greatest adventure isn't travel. It's love. It's family. And it's what I want now."

He smiles as wide as any bride or groom who has ever graced the pages of this magazine, and that's when I know our guest editor has found it—true and everlasting love. The kind of love that fairy tales are made of. The kind of love that makes him want to unpack his suitcase and settle in for the adventure of a lifetime.

Henry Aston, the man whose name is synonymous with *Wanderlust*, is ready to come home.

A tear dropped onto the page, blurring Henry's beautiful words. Everly concentrated on breathing in and out as the ink dissolved into a dark pool.

What had she done?

Henry had said these things weeks ago—before he knew about the babies, before they'd slept together again. He hadn't come back to New York simply to work on Everly's magazine. He'd come back for *her*.

Looking back, she could see it—the care he'd taken with her, the way he'd tried to show her how he felt. Day by day, night by night, kiss by kiss. Henry had always been one of the most patient people Everly had ever met. He'd never been the type to rush into something, and he knew Everly well enough to realize that she hadn't been ready to hear the things he longed to say to her. She'd just been left at the altar. Everly hadn't been in a place where she trusted herself to make a decision about what to have for lunch, never mind making a commitment to love, honor and cherish someone.

So he'd chosen actions over words, and Everly had been too blind to see it. How had she ever allowed Gregory to convince her that Henry wasn't a family man when she'd watched her best friend live out his own father's hopes and dreams for the past decade? He'd wanted to make his dad proud and honor the man who'd raised him. If that wasn't a family man, Everly didn't know what was.

Grief shattered her as the full ramification of what she'd done pressed down her, stealing her breath. Stealing her hope. She really had broken Henry's heart. She'd stolen his chance to experience her pregnancy alongside her. She'd told him he was going to have twins, and then she'd run away...just like Gregory had done to her.

Holly let out a mournful whine and dropped her dainty head onto the toe of Everly's shoe.

"I know, girl. I have to fix this," Everly said through her tears.

But how?

She clutched the pages of the interview to her chest, wishing with all her might that there was some way to undo the damage she'd done...some way to piece Henry's heart back together so they could be a real family. So, as Henry had so eloquently put it, they could "settle in for the adventure of a lifetime."

A single sheet of paper fell from the stack and drifted to the floor. Holly pounced on it, grabbed the corner of page with her teeth and ripped a chunk off the corner of the paper.

"Holly, no," Everly said. "Don't eat Henry's words."

Then her breath caught in her throat, and her fist tightened around the snippet of paper she'd just rescued from Holly's little mouth.

Henry's words.

Everly and Henry were writers. They'd learned to string words together working alongside each other, and it was still what they did, all these years later. When all else failed, they'd always have language. They'd always have words.

Everly suddenly knew what she had to do. She

wasn't sure it would work, but she had to try. She had to tell Henry how she really and truly felt. She needed to give him the words, and some things were just easier to say on the page than they were to utter out loud.

Especially when it came to making amends.

Everly wrote like the wind. She walked out of the fashion closet, went straight to her desk and began pounding away at her keyboard in her lemon sweatpants with her dog in her lap at her cubicle.

There were a few whispers and more than a few stares, but Everly had become accustomed to being the topic of office gossip by then. She didn't glance up from her work until it was finished, ignoring all three of Daphne's attempts to brush her hair and redo her bun, as well as the look of complete and utter horror that Colette shot her way once word had spread that Everly had brought a dog to work and appeared to be engrossed in some mystery assignment.

Once the piece was done and Everly had proofread it twice through a veil of tears, she committed the ultimate office sin at *Veil*: she breezed into Colette's office *without an appointment*.

The editorial assistant parked directly outside Colette's door made a valiant attempt at stopping her, but Everly was too quick. By the time the assistant caught up with her, she was already slapping her pages down in the center of Colette's white, white desk.

Colette looked Everly up and down, from the top

of her badly coiffed head to the tips of her plain white sneakers. She made a *hmph* noise that sort of sounded like Holly when she ate her kibble too fast.

"So sorry, Colette. I tried to stop her," the assistant panted. "Everly doesn't have an appointment."

Everly held her breath. If she got kicked out of the editor in chief's office, so be it. She'd done what she'd needed to do. The article was on Colette's desk. Now she just needed her to read it, preferably right this second.

"It's fine. Everly can stay." Colette sighed. "Leave us to chat in private, please?"

The assistant nodded, scurried out of Colette's office, and then it was just the three of them— Everly, her boss and Everly's heart carefully carved out of her chest and presented to Colette on a silver platter in the form of a Lovebirds column titled "What to Do when You Fall in Love with Your Man of Honor."

Colette looked down at the pages and frowned. "What's this? Everly, we've had this discussion before. You're not working on Lovebirds anymore. I expected two hundred words on groomsmen socks today."

Groomsman socks—now that was a riveting topic. Everly wasn't even allowed to write about dog weddings anymore. She'd be lucky if Colette let her cover hamster nuptials these days.

"I'll get to the groomsmen socks, I promise. But I wanted to try something new for the column. It's an autobiographical piece, and I think after all the press about my wedding a few months ago, this might really get some clicks on the digital site." Everly had thought long and hard about how to properly market the idea when she presented it to Colette and figured she may as well take advantage of her bridal notoriety. It was worth a shot, anyway. "Just please read it. Please, Colette. I'm begging you."

At the sound of the word *beg*, Holly promptly sat up on her back haunches and pawed at the air.

Colette's expertly lined lips twitched into a reluctant smile. "Did you two practice this pitch?"

"No." Everly bit her lip. "I've just spending a lot of time at home lately, and I may have been taught her a few commands."

"Well, it's cute. Dogs still aren't allowed at the office—you know that, right?" Colette asked, smiling full-on now at Holly.

"Understood." Everly nodded. "I'll take her straight home as soon as you read my piece."

Colette's eyebrows lifted. "I take it you're not going to leave my office until I do?"

"Correct."

"Okay, then." Colette waved toward the office chairs situated opposite her. "Have a seat."

Everly collapsed into the chair, too relieved to utter anything besides a quiet "Thank you." Holly leaped into the matching seat, curled into a ball and promptly started snoring. Colette was immediately so absorbed by what Everly had written that she didn't even seem to notice.

Eleven excruciating minutes later, Colette looked up from the pages and fixed her gaze with Everly's. "Is all of this true? Every single word?"

Everly nodded. "Every single word. I promise."

"Well, no wonder you haven't been yourself around the office lately. How is the pregnancy progressing? Are you feeling all right?"

"Other than a serious case of heartbreak, I'm feeling just fine," Everly said.

"Let's see what we can do to help that, shall we?" Colette arched an eyebrow at her.

Everly's chest tightened with anticipation. "I'm sorry...what do you mean, exactly? Are you going to run the piece on the digital site under the Lovebirds banner?"

"I'm going to do you one better than that. I'm going to publish it online just under the masthead. It's good, Everly. It's really good—the best writing I've ever seen from you." Colette stood and offered Everly her hand. "Congratulations on your first feature article for *Veil*."

The tears came hot and fast. Everly nearly fell over herself in an attempt to shake Colette's hand. "Does this mean I can have my column back?"

"Indeed it does." Colette held up a finger. "Strictly on a trial basis. The second you tell a bride to run screaming in the opposite direction of the church, I'm taking you off it again."

"Yes, ma'am. I don't think that will be a problem going forward, though." Everly swallowed around the knot in her throat. "I think I've found my belief in true love."

Colette glanced down at the pages from Everly's article, and her expression went uncharacteristically soft. "It certainly looks that way."

"I don't know how to thank you for this, Colette," Everly said.

Colette shot an indignant glance at Everly's messy bun. "You can start by going home and getting yourself together as soon as you've emailed me your copy. Do it now." Her gaze swiveled toward Holly. "Your dog can stay."

Everly felt her eyes go wide. "I beg your pardon."

"Not *here*, obviously. And not now. I mean at the office in general. You're free to bring her to work if it suits you," Colette said.

"I'd like that very much."

Colette made a shooing motion. "Now go. I have work to do."

"Yes, ma'am." Everly beamed at her boss.

For the first time in weeks, a glimmer of hope stirred deep in her soul. She didn't expect Henry to fall down on one knee and ask her to marry him or anything. That was too much to hope for, too much to even let herself dream about. What she wanted most of all was forgiveness—and maybe, if she was very, very lucky, she'd one day be able to call him her best friend again. It wasn't everything, but it was enough…for now.

Maybe someday they'd find their way back to each other. Maybe time would lessen the hurt, and Henry would be up for the adventure of a lifetime. Maybe not. Either way, she just wanted him back in her life again.

However he'd have her.

Henry was shoving his belongings into his bags when his phone pinged with an incoming text message. Checkout time was in less than half an hour, and he was already cutting it close, but he reached for the phone just in case.

Colette's name flashed on his screen, once again dashing his hopes of hearing from Everly. His jaw clenched, and he almost didn't open the text. He wasn't sure why he did, other than the fact that he'd practically grown roots in his hotel room.

The message didn't contain anything but a link to an article on the *Veil* site. Henry clicked, fully expecting a teaser post about the upcoming June issue, but that's not what it was. Not by a long shot.

What To Do When You Fall In Love With Your Man Of Honor by Everly England.

Henry read the headline three times just to be sure he wasn't imagining things. Hope was a tricky business. No matter how dire things looked and felt between him and Everly in the past few weeks, Henry's hope had never fully dimmed. It was always there, flickering its eternal light in the utter darkness of his soul. He'd never believed things were fully over between them. How could they be? He and Everly were friends first, friends to the end.

And this wasn't the way love stories ended. Period.

Still, he blinked hard, wanting to make sure he wasn't manufacturing something he wanted so desperately to see. But the words were still there in bold lettering, stealing his breath and making him sway on his feet.

He shoved his bag to the side and sank down on the bed. The phone shook in his hands, blurring the type. Henry took a deep breath and read on…

A few months ago, my wedding fell apart in spectacular fashion, but that was only the beginning. The bigger, more spectacular mess was the one I made when I fell in love with my best friend and man of honor.

I can't pinpoint exactly when it happened, but if the past few months have taught me anything, it's that I was in love with Henry long before my wedding day. I think I've been in love with him since college. I just let fear get in the way of accepting the truth, and that's been my biggest mistake of all. Far bigger than the uncut wedding cake or losing my column in this very magazine…

Henry closed his eyes and let Everly's words sink in for several long minutes before continuing. She loved him, and she'd said so, right there in black and white. He'd known how she felt about him for quite some time now, but he hadn't realized how badly he'd needed to hear her say so until right then, sitting all alone in the hotel where it had all started.

He felt like he might break. He wasn't sure how he'd held things together these past weeks knowing Everly was carrying his twins and he couldn't be there. Couldn't kiss her baby bump and tell her everything was going to be okay. Couldn't whisper sweet nothings in her ear at night as he kissed her, loved her, planned their life together. It had been torturous, but he'd tried his best to stay strong and hold the faith. To believe in their future, even when Everly was too afraid to believe in it herself.

And now all it had taken was a simple admission to make him come undone.

I fell in love with my best friend.

Henry's throat thickened as he opened his eyes and forced himself to read the rest. He marveled at each and every word. The article was a how-to guide told in reverse. She implored her readers not to make the same mistakes she'd made. In trying to not to lose the most important friendship she'd ever had, she'd lost something far more precious—the love of her life.

The article was Everly in her truest, most unguarded self. It was the version of Everly that she'd only ever shown Henry and no one else—the girl he'd known and loved for years. Vulnerable. Scared. Real. And by the end, she made it clear that she'd penned the words in an attempt to write herself back into his heart...

Didn't Everly know, though? Couldn't she see? She'd still been there all along.

Colette was true to her word and got Everly's article uploaded to the *Veil* digital site almost as soon as Everly left the office. By the time she reached her apartment, her phone had pinged with alerts, emails and text messages more times than she could count. Every time her cell chimed, fear splintered her heart as she tapped on the notification to read who it was from.

Friends, colleagues and people she hardly knew were reaching out to her, one right after the next, to tell her how touched they'd been by her article.

We're all pulling for you and Henry, Daphne texted.

He'll come home. I know he will, Addison added, which prompted instant tears.

Even Jack King, Daphne's fact-checking nemesis sent Everly a message through their interoffice Slack channel. Wonderful work, Everly. Everyone at Veil is glad to have you back on your column.

Everyone had something lovely to say...

Everyone, that is, except the one person she wanted to hear from most of all.

"He'll see it, won't he, Holly?" Everly whispered into her sweet dog's ear as she unlocked the front door. Once inside, she released Holly and the Cavalier's furry paws scrambled for purchase on the smooth marble floor.

The dog pranced a circle around Everly and then plopped onto her bottom and stared up at her, tail swishing. They were home, but it didn't much feel like it. Not anymore.

Everly stood for a second in the entryway to the apartment, looking around at the place where she'd grown up. This was the home where her parents had built a family. Built a life. When she'd inherited the apartment, she'd always thought she'd do the same someday. She just never imagined she'd be doing it all on her own.

It wasn't supposed to be this way. Everly had never imagined being pregnant without the man she loved by her side, painting the nursery together, buying tiny socks and sweet little outfits, smiling with giddy anticipation. Never imagined a time when she and Henry wouldn't be on speaking terms. Never imagined hurting him the way she'd done.

Regret burned in the pit of her stomach. Did she really think she could write her way out of this? She'd broken Henry's heart. Words couldn't repair that kind of damage—not when she'd stolen so much from him. She'd taken every memory they'd built together and acted as if none of it mattered. She'd reduced their relationship to playing house. He'd never place his hand on her belly and feel the babies' kicks. He was going to miss everything, and worst of all, she'd never even given him the chance to tell her that's what he wanted most of all. He'd wanted a future with her more than anything else, more than the world itself.

He'd tried to tell her, hadn't he? The night they'd made love, he'd put his heart right out there for the taking.

I just want to touch you...love you. Will you let me do that, darling? Just for us this time. Not to make you forget anyone else or to remind yourself that you're desirable. Because you are, E. I desire you. Always have, always will.

Everly hadn't heard those words. Not really. She'd let them flutter over her like butterfly kisses, but she hadn't truly taken them in. It was no wonder he didn't want anything to do with her anymore.

If only she could make him read the article, maybe she could make him understand that she'd never really wanted him to go. She'd simply let fear get the better of her, the same way she always did.

She couldn't do that anymore. No matter what happened with Henry—even if she never saw him again—she couldn't live that way. Addison had been right. Everly wanted to love with her heart wide open, and the only way to do that was to allow herself to be loved right back. Anything else wasn't real.

She took a deep breath and focused on Holly staring up at her as if she'd just hung the moon. *People could learn a thing or two from dogs about love, couldn't they?* Holly's tail wagged even harder.

Everly's spirits lifted just a bit. "The article just went up a few minutes ago. Surely he'll see it eventually."

"He already did," a voice said from somewhere inside the apartment.

Everly's heart nearly stopped. Was she hearing things?

Please let this be real. Please.

Holly cocked her head, ears pricked forward. So she *wasn't* hearing things…

Everly took a shaky inhale.

"Henry?" she called out through a sob. She pressed her fingertips to her lips in an effort to keep her emotions at bay, but there was no use. She was already ugly crying, and she'd yet to even set eyes on him.

"I'm in here, darling. Where else would I be?" he said, and Holly took off like a shot toward Everly's bathroom.

Everly smiled through her tears as she followed Holly's wagging tail. When she reached the bathroom, she found Henry sitting on the floor with his legs stretched out in front of him, feet crossed languidly at the ankles as he leaned against the bathtub. A box of Ritz Crackers sat beside him, and he had a can of squirt cheese in his hand.

The relief that coursed through her at the sight of him nearly made her knees buckle. He'd come back. He was *here,* and no matter what happened next, at least she'd have a chance to tell him to his face how much she'd missed him. How much she adored him.

She laughed despite herself. "Am I hallucinating? Is this really happening?"

"This is real life, darling. *Our* life. I figured if we're going to start over, we should do it the same way we started the first time," he said, and suddenly, his voice was infused with emotion, same as hers.

A bittersweet smile creased his face, he opened his arms and in a flash, Everly was straddling his lap, kissing him like she'd just gotten a second chance she'd been too afraid to imagine. One that she didn't think she fully deserved.

"I love you," she whispered against the scruff on his jawline. "I love you so much, Henry."

"I love you, too, darling," he said with a sweet, sweet ache in his voice. "Always have, always will."

"You read my story? All of it?" she asked. There was so much to say, but suddenly talking was the last thing she wanted to do. They'd both said everything they needed to say on paper, for all the world to see.

Now she just wanted to make up for all the time they'd lost. To think they could have been together like this for years if only she'd been brave enough to let herself fall.

But she hadn't been ready back then. Now, she

was. They both were, and just like every treasured memory of the past eight years of knowing Henry, this one was happening right when it was supposed to. This was their time. This was their happy-ever-after—not an ending, but a beginning. A more beautiful beginning than she could've dreamed of, especially all those years ago when she and Henry first met.

That was the beauty of falling in love with your best friend, though. Looking back, it all made so much sense. Henry had been her man of honor all along.

His gaze dropped lower, and when he caught sight of the silver charms on her necklace, his face cracked into her favorite lopsided grin. "What's this? E and H?"

He toyed with the silver charms, blue eyes glittering like an endless, open sky.

"It's us. Me and you, Everly and Henry. Forever." Everly bit her lip as she . "But you might owe Holly a little blue box of her own now She still needs a charm for her collar."

At the sound of her name, the little dog yipped. Her happy bark echoed off the marble walls as she tried to wiggle her way between Everly and Henry and join in on the reunion.

"Done." Henry laughed then brought the charms to his lips and pressed a kiss to the silver initials.

"If you're still up for the adventure of a lifetime,

I'm ready to help you unpack your bags," Everly whispered. She'd practiced the words in her head over and over again, and still her heart was so full of emotion that she could barely get them out.

The look Henry gave her in response made her feel like she could finally breathe again after weeks of holding her breath. "Good, because I'm not going to Antarctica."

"You're not?" Joy filled Everly like sunshine. She'd thought he might say this, but hearing it was almost too good to be true.

"No, I'm not. I never wanted to leave, silly." He placed a reverent hand on her baby bump as Holly craned her neck to lick the side of his face. "I'm going to stay right here with the ones I love. In fact, I've got a little secret of my own. Do you want to hear it?"

Everly shifted so she could study his expression. Whatever the secret was, he seemed eager to share it. "Yes, please."

"I've resigned from *Wanderlust* and accepted a job as the new permanent travel editor at *Veil*. I suggested it to Colette and she agreed right away. I was just about to check out of the Plaza so I could come and tell you when I saw the article. I was planning on beating your door down if I had to. Luckily, that no longer seemed necessary. Even luckier, I still had my key. Darling, I'm officially home to stay." He pulled Everly close and began kissing his way down her neck. And everything that she'd been holding on to for so long—all the fears, all the hurt, all the grief—melted away. He was her man of honor, now and forever more. "Looks like you're stuck with me, E."

Until death do they part…

Epilogue

Veil Magazine, June Issue
Wedding Report

Veil's own Everly England and Henry Aston tied the knot this month in a private ceremony in the Conservatory Garden at Central Park, Manhattan. The bride wore a bespoke retro-inspired gown by Givenchy. The ballerina-length creation featured a bateau neckline, a full tulle skirt and a drop-waist satin bodice. The design was a collaboration between the bride and the French fashion house, drawing inspiration from the Givenchy wedding dress worn by Audrey Hepburn in the film *Funny Face*. The groom wore black tie by Armani.

Surrounded by only close friends and family, the

happy couple exchanged vows near the Three Dancing Maidens fountain in the Conservatory's North Garden, a spot of significant meaning to the bride and groom. The ceremony was an intimate affair, with the only attendant being the Cavalier King Charles spaniel the couple shares, who goes by the name Holly Golightly. Holly wore a floral wreath around her neck, crafted from blush peonies and pink cherry blossoms.

After the ceremony, guests enjoyed a champagne reception at the Plaza Hotel, where the newly married couple later spent their first night together as man and wife, special guests of the Plaza's luxurious honeymoon suite.

Everly England is the author of *Veil*'s popular Lovebirds column and has recently been promoted to Features Editor. Henry Aston is the magazine's new Travel Editor. After a brief honeymoon in Antigua, the couple will make their home in New York City. Everly and Henry are thrilled to announce that they are expecting twins in October.

Everyone here at *Veil* wishes them a long, happy, adventurous life together.

* * * * *

Looking for more friends to lovers romances?
Try these swoonworthy romances from
Harlequin Special Edition:

The Rancher's Baby
By Kathy Douglass

Her Best Friend's Baby
By Tara Taylor Quinn

A Fortune's Windfall
By Michelle Major

Available now wherever Harlequin Special Edition
books and ebooks are sold!

SPECIAL EXCERPT FROM

Read on for a sneak preview of
Faking a Fairy Tale,
The next book in USA TODAY *bestselling*
author Teri Wilson's Love Unveiled series,
coming September 2023!

Chapter One

Fashion closet. Now!

Daphne Ballantyne's glitter-manicured finger-tips tapped out the frantic group text as she rushed past a rolling rack full of designer wedding gowns. Head bent over her phone, a wisp of gossamer-thin, embellished fabric hit her in the face—just another occupational hazard of working at *Veil*, Manhattan's premiere bridal magazine.

Daphne brushed the organza aside, stilettos clicking on the smooth marble floor as she rushed toward the fashion closet in a whirl of furious, sparkling indignation. Jack King had done it again, and this time, he'd really gone too far. Daphne was going to lose it, albeit in exquisitely groomed fashion.

As the magazine's beauty editor, it was Daphne's

job to keep up with the latest trends in cosmetics, skin care and body care, and Daphne did so with unbridled enthusiasm. Just this morning, she'd added fresh sparkles to her hair with the bedazzling tool that had gone viral online after she'd featured the device in the June issue of *Veil*. This evening, she had an appointment after work to get new eyelash extensions. Daphne was in the middle of writing a feature on various lash options for brides and had been offered a trial run from a popular salon in Chelsea that had styles ranging from the demure, understated Blushing Bride all the way to the dramatic Bridezilla. Daphne fully intended to take the Bridezilla lashes for a spin. Go big or go home.

First, though, she had a war to wage right here at *Veil*.

"What happened? Is everything okay?" Addison England, the magazine's deputy editor and one-third of the trio of best friends who called themselves the *Veil crew,* was already ready and waiting when Daphne stormed into the fashion closet.

Everly England—Addison's younger sister, who'd recently been promoted to features editor—breezed in right on Daphne's heels.

"Of course the pregnant lady is the last one to get here. What I did I miss?" Everly asked, gaze swiveling back and forth between Daphne and Addison as she rested a gentle hand on her ever-expanding belly.

"Nothing…" Addison said with a shrug. "…*yet*. We just got here too."

The sisters both turned curious eyes on Daphne. "Spill," they said in unison.

Daphne hadn't expressly stated that she was currently in crisis mode when she'd fired off the group text message. The urgency of her situation had been a given, because the words *fashion closet* said it all.

The *Veil* closet was an enormous space within the magazine's sleek, Upper East Side headquarters where articles of clothing that had either been gifted or loaned to *Veil* were stored with meticulous care. Couture wedding gowns and bridesmaids dresses hung from the maze of rolling racks crisscrossing the closet. The walls were lined with shelves upon shelves of designer shoes and custom drawers containing wedding veils stitched from fine organza, illusion tulle and exquisitely crafted Burano lace. Somewhere among the miles of bridal white fluff was a small collection of bespoke men's tuxedos… supposedly. None of the *Veil* crew had actually set eyes on it, but rumors of its existence abounded.

Daphne couldn't remember exactly when or how the fashion closet had become a place of refuge for her, Addison and Everly. But whenever one of them needed a shoulder to cry on or just a place to vent, they gathered on the closet's enormous white silk damask tufted ottoman. It was hard to be upset surrounded by all of those exquisite gowns. Being in the closet always made Daphne feel just a little bit like a princess—even today when she was royally ticked-off.

"It's *him*." Daphne fumed. "Again."

"Oh, boy. This is going to take a while, isn't it?" Everly kicked off her Audrey Hepburn-esque ballerina flats and lowered herself onto the ottoman. For a woman who was expecting twins in less than two months, she still moved with an impressive amount of grace.

"What did Jack do this time?" Addison said as she picked an invisible speck of link from her ivory and black tweed skirt suit.

Was it Daphne's imagination or was her girl gang acting unusually blasé about her state of unease?

Daphne crossed her arms and shot an indignant glance at her friends. "Neither of you seems to be taking this very seriously."

"We are." Everly nodded with a yawn. "*So* seriously."

"I'm going to overlook the yawn because you're with child and all, but you—" Daphne's gaze swiveled toward Addison, who was now inspecting her perfectly polished nails. The color looked like Essie's Ballet Slippers, a favorite of brides the world over. Daphne would've bet her entire paycheck on it. "—where's your sense of outrage on my behalf?"

"First of all…" Addison raised a single Ballet Slip-per-tipped finger. "…you haven't even told us what he did yet. And second…"

Everly finished for her. "Jack isn't such a bad person. He sent me a really nice text when my first feature article went live. Everyone in the office seems to like him."

Daphne arched an irate brow. "With one very notable exception."

"Everly is just trying to explain that we don't quite understand why you two can't seem to get along," Addison said.

"This." Daphne slapped the yellow post-it note she'd been clenching in one of her fists down onto the ottoman. "*This* is why."

Addison and Everly leaned over the offending square of paper and peered down at it.

Daphne smoothed the creases out of the post-it until Jack's annoyingly perfect penmanship was clearly legible. Then there they were, his four favorite words in all of the English language.

We can't print this.

Everly frowned. "Did he shoot down another of your articles?"

"Yes, he most definitely did. And this time, he didn't even have the decency to email me an explanation. He just stuck a post-it on my pages and left them on my chair for me to find first thing this morning." Daphne's head hurt. She couldn't deal with this before her morning cup of coffee.

Although, Addison always joked that Daphne put so much flavored creamer in her brew that it no longer resembled actual coffee. Whatever. All Daphne knew was that there was a mug of cookies-and-cream flavored caffeinated beverage sitting in her cubicle, waiting to be consumed. She just needed to eviscerate Jack King first.

Metaphorically speaking, of course.

"This is the third time he's pulled one of my articles," Daphne said.

"That's really not so bad, Daph." Everly shrugged. "He's been at *Veil* for at least five months by now."

"The third time *this week*," Daphne clarified.

"Ouch." Everly winced. "Point taken."

At long last, Addison cast Daphne a properly sympathetic look. "I can see why that would be frustrating."

She had no idea.

Daphne sighed and glanced from Addison to Everly and back again as she collapsed into a dejected heap on the ottoman. "How many times has he done this to you two?"

"Actually, he's never pulled one of my articles," Addison said.

Everly shrugged. "Me either."

Daphne wanted to scream into one of the white satin ring pillows stacked on the shelf immediately to her right. "You've *got* to be kidding me."

And just like that, she was on her feet again, pacing around the cramped space. For some reason, all the bridal white taffeta, airy organza and shiny little beads were doing nothing to calm her nerves this morning. When couture fashion and a bit of sparkle failed to make Daphne feel better, she knew there was something seriously wrong.

"He's making me crazy." She threw her arms in the air, narrowly missing a Monique Lhuillier mesh tulle dress with blue floral appliqué.

Daphne paused for a beat to admire it. She *refused* to let Jack steal her appreciation for a wedding dress with a touch of color. If Daphne ever got married, she wanted her gown to look like a designer puff of pastel cotton candy.

Not that she had any intention of walking down the aisle in the foreseeable future. Maybe not ever.

"Daph, you know I adore you, but fact checking is Jack's job," Addison, ever the voice of reason, said. "It's right there in his title: fact checker. If every word of an article can't be verified, he has no choice but to intervene."

Daphne knew this, of course. She'd been working at *Veil* for a decade already, straight out of high school. She'd started off working the night shift with the cleaning crew while she attended community college classes during the day in Astoria, where she'd still lived at home with her dad. The moment she'd set foot in the glamorous office, Daphne knew she wanted to work on the staff someday. She spun stories in her head about the beautiful gowns she spied hanging in the fashion closet while she emptied the trash bins and dusted cubicles. To her father's bemusement, she started reading the *Vows* section of The New York Times, learning everything she could about weddings and bridal fashion. And when the time came to choose a major at school, Daphne selected journalism without the slightest hesitation.

When a receptionist job at *Veil* became available during her junior year, she spent every spare dime she had on a knock-off Chanel suit and all but begged Colette Winter, *Veil's* editor-in-chief, for the position during her interview. It paid even less than her cleaning job, but the first time she took a seat behind the magazine's glossy white reception desk, Daphne cried actual tears of joy. She'd done it—she was a *Veil* girl.

She finished her degree by switching to night classes. Three years after taking the receptionist job, she got promoted to an assistant position and she'd been working her way farther up the glittery, glamorous ladder at *Veil* ever since. Sometimes she had to pinch herself to believe how far she'd come. Other days, all it took was a simple post-it note to remind her that, unlike the rest of the staff, she hadn't gone to a fancy Ivy League university or grown up on the Upper West Side.

Perhaps she reading too much into her ongoing battle with Jack King. Then again, maybe she wasn't.

"I knew it." Daphne felt like crying. Either that, or strangling a certain fact checker. "He's targeting me."

"I really doubt that. Fact checking is a touchy business. Also—" Addison pulled a face. "—you two might want to at least *try* and get along. People are starting to talk."

Daphne blinked. Seriously? Everyone at the magazine loved her. Almost everyone, anyway. "What people?"

"Literally everyone in the building," Everly oh-so-helpfully added. "We've all heard you and Jack arguing about your copy."

"It's only a matter of time until Colette notices, and you know how she feels about staff members not getting along." Addison bit her lip.

As much as Daphne loathed to admit it, Addison was right. Their editor-in-chief ran a tight ship, and Colette was fundamentally opposed to anything that disrupted the workplace.

Everly nodded. "If there's one thing Colette hates, it's drama."

"And sensible shoes," Addison said.

"And casual Fridays," Everly added.

Addison arched a knowing eyebrow. "And white after Labor Day."

They were getting way off track. Daphne didn't need help writing a listicle about Colette's likes and dislikes. She needed Jack to leave her alone. Or, preferably, to leave altogether and take a job someplace else—like *Robot Monthly*, maybe, since he had about as much personality as a washing machine.

Daphne had never once seen the man smile. Nor had he ever take a single bite of the wedding cake samples that popped up from time to time in the break room. What kind of monster didn't like *cake?*

Daphne groaned. "What am I going to do?"

"For right now, I think it's best to just lay low and do whatever it takes to get along with the guy. I know you think he's impossible, but Colette loves him, and the last thing you want is to get on her bad side for any reason whatsoever." Everly shot her a meaningful look. "Trust me on this."

"I hear you," Daphne said. She had, after all, witnessed every painful moment of Everly's recent struggles at work. Colette had even demoted Everly for a while, but Everly had risen to the top, just like cream. Because she loved her job.

Just like Daphne loved hers. She couldn't let Jack ruin things at *Veil* for her. She wouldn't.

"Okay, the new game plan is to smother Jack with sweetness," she said. She couldn't keep bickering with him if everyone in the office was chattering about their feud. It wasn't as if all the quarreling was doing any good, anyway.

Addison's eyes narrowed. "You don't mean smother him in the literal sense, do you?"

"No, of course not." Although the idea wasn't without its appeal.

"Good, just checking," Addison said.

"You should also avoid Colette at all costs until things settle down between you and Jack." Everly folded her arms over her pregnant belly. "Just saying."

Daphne took in a deep breath. "Done."

Then the door to the fashion closet swung open, and Colette's assistant rushed inside. When her gaze landed on Daphne, the assistant's slim shoulders sagged in relief. "Oh, good. Here you are."

"Me?" Daphne's hand fluttered to her heart. She swallowed, fervently hoping there was some invisible person standing behind her.

Alas, there wasn't.

"Yes. You, Daphne." The assistant waved her toward the door. "I've been looking everywhere for you. Colette wants to see you in her office right away."

"Oh, she does? Great." *So, so great.* This couldn't be good. Daphne's legs went wobbly as she stood and smoothed down the front of her retro-inspired dress. The bubblegum pink fabric was decorated with tubes of lipstick and bright red kiss marks. Her career might be on the brink of going down in flames, but at least she'd look cute as it burned.

She shot a parting wave at Addison and Everly, who'd both gone slightly wide-eyed.

Text us, Everly mouthed.

Daphne nodded. *Will do.*

As she followed Colette's assistant toward the editor-in-chief's office, Daphne concentrated on breathing in and out, just like she'd advised nervous brides to do in the article she'd written last month called *Say I Do to Pre-Wedding Yoga.* Jack had made her omit two full paragraphs from that piece, because of course he had.

Stop thinking about him, her subconscious screamed. *He's utterly unimportant to your life or your career.*

That last part wasn't quite true, though. If she wasn't careful, Jack and his irritating pad of post-it notes could fully torpedo her standing at *Veil…*

But only if Daphne let him.

She took in a ragged, non-yoga-like breath as she passed the cubicle area of the office. A few curious faces swiveled in her direction, and she forced herself to hold her head high. Whatever Colette wanted probably had nothing whatsoever to do with their ongoing feud. The last time Daphne had been unexpectedly summoned to her boss's office, she'd been offered a promotion. *And* a raise. This was probably a good thing. She really needed to stop letting Jack get inside her head like this.

Except the second she stepped through the doorway of Colette's office, she realized all her efforts to forget about Jack would be futile. He wasn't just in her head…he was right there, sitting across the cream-colored lacquer desk from their boss with his annoying backside planted in one of Colette's faux fur white chairs.

Daphne wished she hadn't noticed that his backside, while every bit as annoying as the rest of him, also looked quite nice in a tailored suit. Unfortunately, she'd come to that realization on his very first day at the magazine. His chiseled face wasn't any less appealing, even though the set of his jaw was typically so hard that it looked as if his pearly white molars could cut coal into diamonds with minimal effort.

Stop thinking about him, she repeated to herself. *And* definitely *stop thinking about his backside.*

What was wrong with her?

Daphne stood rooted to the spot. One thing was clear: this meeting wasn't about a promotion. Quite possibly, it was about the opposite. Colette had certainly demoted people before. If ever there was a time to smother Jack King with kindness, it was right here and now, while the editor-in-chief was watching.

Jack swiveled in his chair, glittering gray eyes settling on Daphne with a perfectly inscrutable expression. The man was dead inside. She managed to paste a smile on her face, but it felt more like a snarl. Then the corner of his mouth twitched into a reluctant looking half-grin. Super. Stony-faced Jack King, lover of obscure facts and hater of cake was *laughing* at her.

Daphne smiled so hard that her head hurt.

What was *he* doing here?

What was *she* doing here?

Jack King blinked against the assault of glitter sparkling at him from Daphne Ballantyne's hair. As per usual, the beauty editor looked like she'd had a run-in with a chandelier on her way to work. Also as per usual, she was glaring at him as if he'd just kicked a puppy.

Jack hadn't kicked a puppy, obviously. Never had and never would. Not that Daphne cared, as she seemed to have somewhat of a loose relationship with actual facts.

"Jack," she said as she took the seat beside him. For some reason, she appeared to be trying her best to smile at him. Clearly it pained her.

Jack couldn't help feeling the slightest bit amused. Was that an immature reaction? Probably. Then again, Daphne herself hadn't exactly been a beacon of professionalism yesterday when she'd barged into his office, accused him of being a control freak and purposely rearranged his carefully organized office supplies in an attempt to rattle him.

Jack had definitely been rattled. Fine, he could admit it: he liked things orderly and predictable. Was that really such a bad thing? And the last time he checked, neatness was a positive trait in the workplace. Daphne might want to try it sometime. Earlier this morning, when Jack tried to stick a post-it note to her desk, there hadn't been a square inch of available space to affix it to. Her cubicle was filled to overflowing with makeup brushes, cosmetics, hair products and more bottles of hand lotion than he could count. And glitter! Glitter *everywhere*.

Jack had very carefully pressed the post-it note to her pages and left them on the seat of Daphne's chair. Even so, he'd somehow found himself plucking specks of glitter from his necktie half an hour later.

"Daphne," Jack said to her in return. He stood while she took her seat, because in addition to liking things neat and orderly, Jack also had manners.

"Oh, were you just leaving?" Daphne asked as he towered over her. Her smile suddenly seemed more genuine.

"No." Jack sat back down, spine ramrod straight. "I was simply being polite."

She snorted and then tried to cover it with a cough.

Jack's jaw involuntarily clenched. The woman was a bewitching, bedazzled thorn in his side. He truly didn't know why he let her get to him the way that she did.

He swiveled to face forward, focusing all of this attention on Colette. Still, Daphne shimmered in his periphery, about as easy to ignore as a disco ball.

"Good morning," Colette said. She folded her hands on the surface of her pristine, cream-colored desk. There wasn't a laptop or even a pen in sight—only a tasteful bouquet of white roses in a vase on the desk's far right-hand corner. Minimalism at its finest. With any luck, Daphne was taking notes.

"Morning, Colette," Daphne gushed beside him.

Jack cleared his throat. "Good day."

A trickle of unease snaked its way up his spine as Colette's gaze flicked back and forth between them. What was the purpose of this meeting, exactly?

"Thank you for coming in. There's something very important I need to discuss with both of you," Colette said.

"Yes, of course," Daphne said.

Jack remained silent. He was beginning to get a bad feeling about where this conversation could possibly be headed.

"How would you say the two of you get along?" Colette asked.

And there it was.

He and Daphne had been hauled into the editor-in-chief's office like two schoolchildren who'd been ordered to see the principal. Jack didn't know whether to be mortified or furious.

Both.

Definitely both.

This wasn't him. Jack took his job seriously. He didn't engage in petty work squabbles. In prep school, he'd been voted "most likely to become a workaholic," and he'd been the top-ranked student in his class at Princeton. His work ethic was legendary.

He was a model employee, damn it. Or he had been…

Until his world had been turned upside-down six months ago.

Jack was getting back on track, though. He really

was. The only visible cracks in his composure came about when Daphne Ballantyne was in the immediate vicinity.

"We get along great." Daphne beamed at him. "Jack is wonderful. *So* fastidious."

He narrowed his gaze at her, ever so slightly. "Yes, we work very well together. Daphne is undeniably... colorful."

They sat staring at each other for a beat, gazes locked in silent warfare. Then Daphne licked her lips, and Jack's attention strayed toward her mouth—accidentally, of course. But for a strange, nonsensical moment, he couldn't bring himself to look away.

"Good, I'm glad to hear it," Colette said.

Focus, Jack's subconscious ordered. He snapped his head back toward his boss, tugging slightly at his shirt collar.

"Because I have to say, I've sensed a bit of animosity between you a time or two, and this is never going to work if that's the case." Colette held up her hands.

"What?" Daphne sputtered out a laugh. "Animosity? No, absolutely not. Honestly, Colette, I'm not sure where this is coming from. Right, Jack?"

"Correct." He gave a wooden nod. Jack had always been a terrible liar—again, something he'd always considered to be a positive attribute.

Not so, if the momentary spark of fury in Daphne's aquamarine eyes was any indication.

She sighed and turned her gaze back to Colette. "Please don't fire us."

Jack pinched the bridge of his nose. They couldn't pretend to like each other for longer than two minutes, even when both of their jobs were at stake. What was this? Kindergarten?

"Fire you?" Colette's brow furrowed. "I'm not following."

"You just said this is never going to work if Jack and I don't get along." There was an unmistakable tremor in Daphne's voice that made Jack's body feel leaden all of a sudden. Or maybe that was simply a by-product of his pending unemployment.

"We can make it work," he said, tongue tripping only slightly on the word *we*. As if the very thought of being part of a collective with Daphne was so inconceivable that his mouth refused to cooperate.

"Still not following." Colette shook her head. "At all. Regardless, I have no intention of firing either of you. You both do excellent work."

Daphne's knee, just out of Colette's sight, gave Jack's thigh a sharp nudge. He could practically hear her internal squeal of triumph. *Did you hear that, Jack? I do excellent work.*

He sighed mightily. What was it going to take to get Colette to cut to the chase so he could get out of here? He longed for the solitude of his office, where his stapler was always situated exactly one inch to the left of his leather desk blotter and he knew exactly what was expected of him from one minute to the next. Fact checking suited him. Verifying information was black and white, with no room for gray. No room for confusion. No room for surprises or chaos.

Which was precisely why he excelled at it.

"Colette, if I may..." Jack said, ignoring Daphne's invisible eye roll in response to his formality. "Clearly there's been some confusion. What is it, precisely, that Daphne and I need to make work?"

"Your engagement," Colette said, as if that made a lick of sense.

"Our w-what?" Daphne sputtered. She'd gone deathly pale, those luminous, blue-green eyes of hers huge in her delicate face.

Jack's chest went so fiercely tight that he couldn't breathe. Maybe they'd both heard Colette wrong. Maybe he'd just had some sort of stress-induced auditory hallucination. Maybe he needed to pack up his stapler and his desk blotter and find a new job.

"I beg your pardon?" he managed to utter.

"Your engagement," Colette repeated, this time with a sense of finality that settled like a rock in the pit of Jack's gut.

He didn't dare look at Daphne. In fact, he preferred to pretend she didn't exist altogether. Whatever this was couldn't be real. In no universe could Daphne Ballantyne be his fiancé.

"I've chosen the two of you to go under cover for

a *Veil* special assignment," Colette said, as if they'd both just won the lottery. Then, oblivious to their mutual suffering, she flashed Jack and Daphne a wink. "Congratulations! You're betrothed."

Don't miss
Faking a Fairy Tale *by Teri Wilson,*
available September 2023 wherever
Harlequin® Special Edition books
and ebooks are sold.
www.Harlequin.com

HARLEQUIN
PLUS

Try the best multimedia
subscription service for romance
readers like you!

Read, Watch and Play.

Experience the easiest way to get
the romance content you crave.

Start your **FREE TRIAL** at
<u>www.harlequinplus.com/freetrial</u>.